Amaryllis at the Fair

Richard Jefferies

Amaryllis at the Fair

The present edition is a reproduction of previous publication of this classic work. Minor typographical errors may have been corrected without note; however, for an authentic reading experience the spelling, punctuation, and capitalization have been retained from the original text.

ISBN: 978-1-64799-586-7

CONTENTS

AMARYLLIS AT THE FAIR

DEDICATED

TO

CHARLES PRESTWICH SCOTT

INTRODUCTION[1]

"THE book is not a novel" is a phrase often in the mouth of critics, who on second thoughts might, perhaps, add with less emphasis, "It does not conform to the common type of novel." Fortified, however, with that sense of rectitude that dictates conformity to our neighbours and a safe acquiescence in the mysterious movements of public taste, the critics have exclaimed with touching unanimity—"What a pity Jefferies tried to write novels! Why didn't he stick to essays in natural history!"

What a pity Jefferies should have given us "Amaryllis at the Fair," and "After London"!—this opinion has been propagated with such fervency that it seems almost a pity to disturb it by inquiring into the nature of these his achievements. Certainly the critics, and their critical echoes, are united. "He wrote some later novels of indifferent merit," says a critic in "Chambers' Encyclopædia." "Has anyone ever been able to write with free and genuine appreciation of even the later novels?" asks or echoes a lady, Miss Grace Toplis, writing on Jefferies. "In brief, he was an essayist and not a novelist at all," says Mr. Henry Salt. "It is therefore certain that his importance for posterity will dwindle, if it has not already dwindled, to that given by a bundle of descriptive selections. But these will occupy a foremost place on their particular shelf, the shelf at the head of which stands Gilbert White and Gray," says Mr. George Saintsbury. "He was a reporter of genius, and he never got beyond reporting. Mr. Besant has the vitalising imagination which Jefferies lacked," says Mr. Henley in his review of Walter Besant's "Eulogy of Richard Jefferies"; and again, "They are not novels as he (Walter Besant) admits, they are a series of pictures. . . . That is the way he takes Jefferies at Jefferies' worst." Yes, it is very touching this unanimity, and it is therefore a pleasure for this critic to say that in his judgment "Amaryllis at the Fair" is one of the very few later-day novels of English country life that are worth putting on one's shelf, and that to make room for it he would turn out certain highly-praised novels by Hardy which do not ring quite true, novels which the critics and the public, again with touching unanimity, have voted to be of high rank. But what is a novel? the reader may ask. A novel, says the learned Charles Annandale, is "a fictitious prose narrative, involving some plot of greater or less intricacy, and

---

[1] Reprinted in part from "The Academy" of April 4th, 1903.

professing to give a picture of real life, generally exhibiting the passions and sentiments, in a state of great activity, and especially the passion of love." Well, "Amaryllis at the Fair" is a fictitious prose narrative professing to give a picture of real life, and involving a plot of little intricacy. Certainly it exhibits the passions and sentiments in a state of great activity. But Mr. Henry Salt, whose little book on Jefferies is the best yet published, further remarks: "Jefferies was quite unable to give any vivid dramatic life to his stories . . . his instinct was that of the naturalist who observes and moralizes rather than that of the novelist who penetrates and interprets; and consequently his rustic characters, though strongly and clearly drawn, do not live, as, for example, those of Thomas Hardy live. . . . Men and animals are alike mere figures in his landscapes."

So far the critics. Jefferies being justly held to be "no ordinary novelist," it is inferred by most that something is wrong with "Amaryllis the Fair," and the book has been passed over in silence. But we do not judge every novel by the same test. We do not judge "Tristram Shandy," for example, by its intricate plot, or by its "vivid drama," we judge it simply as an artistic revelation of human life and by its humorous insight into human character. And judged by the same simple test "Amaryllis at the Fair," we contend, is a living picture of life, a creative work of imagination of a high order. Iden, the unsuccessful farmer who "built for all time, and not for the circumstances of the hour," is a masterly piece of character drawing. But Iden is a personal portrait, the reader may object, Well, what about Uncle Toby? From what void did he spring? Iden, to our mind, is almost as masterly a conception, as broadly human a figure as Uncle Toby. And Mrs. Iden, where will you find this type of nervous, irritable wife, full of spiteful disillusioned love for her dilatory husband better painted than by Jefferies? But Mrs. Iden is a type, not an individual, the reader may say. Excellent reader! and what about the Widow Wadman? She is no less and no more of an individual than is Mrs. Iden. It was a great feat of Sterne to create so cunningly the atmosphere of the Shandy household, but Jefferies has accomplished an artistic feat also in drawing the relations of the Idens, father, mother, and daughter. How true, how unerringly true to human nature is this picture of the Iden household; how delicately felt and rendered to a hair is his picture of the father's sluggish, masculine will, pricked ineffectually by the waspish tongue of feminine criticism. Further, we not only have the family's idiosyncrasies, their habits, mental atmosphere, and domestic story brought before us in a hundred pages, easily and instinctively by the hand of the artist, but we have the whole book steeped in the breath of English spring, the restless ache of spring that thrills through the nerves, and stirs the sluggish winter blood; we have the spring feeling breaking from the March heavens and the March earth in copse, meadow, and ploughland, as it has scarcely been rendered before by English novelist. The description of Amaryllis running out into the March wind to call her father from his potato planting to see the daffodil; the picture of Iden pretending to sleep in his chair that he may watch the mice; the description of the girl Amaryllis watching the crowd of plain, ugly men of the countryside flocking along the road to the fair; the description of Amadis the invalid, in the old farm kitchen among the stalwart country folk—all these pictures and a dozen others in the book are painted with a masterly hand. Pictures! the critical reader may complain. Yes, pictures of living men and women. What does it matter whether a revelation of human life is conveyed to us by pictures or by action so long as it is conveyed? Mr. Saintsbury classes Jefferies with Gray, presumably because both writers have written of the English landscape. With Gray! Jefferies in his work as a naturalist and observer of wild life may be classed merely for convenience with Gilbert White. But this classification only applies to one half of Jefferies' books. By his "Wild Life in a Southern County" he stands beside Gilbert White; by his "Story of My Heart" he stands by himself, a little apart from the poets, and by "Amaryllis at the Fair" he stands among the half-dozen country writers of the century whose work is racy of the English soil and of rural English human nature. We will name three of these writers, Barnes, Cobbett, Waugh, and our attentive readers can name the other three.

To come back to "Amaryllis at the Fair," why is it so masterly, or, further, wherein is it so masterly, the curious reader may inquire? "Is it not full of digressions? Granted that the first half of the 'novel' is beautiful in style, does not Jefferies suddenly break his method, introduce his own personality, intersperse abrupt disquisitions on food, illness, and Fleet Street? Is not that description of Iden's dinner a little—well, a little unusual? In short, is not the book a disquisition on life from the standpoint of Jefferies' personal experiences? And if this is so, how can the book be so fine an achievement?" Oh, candid reader, with the voice of authority sounding in your ears (and have we not Mr. Henley and Mr. Saintsbury bound in critical amity against us), a book may break the formal rules, and yet it may yield to us just that salt of life which we may seek for vainly in the works of more faultless writers. The strength of "Amaryllis at the Fair" is that its beauty springs naturally from the prosaic earthly facts of life it narrates, and that, in the natural atmosphere breathed by its people, the prose and the poetry of their life are one. In the respect of the artistic naturalness of its homely picture, the book is very superior to, say "The Mayor of Casterbridge," where we are conscious that the author has been at work arranging and rearranging his charming studies and impressions of the old-world people of Casterbridge into the pattern of an exciting plot. Now it is precisely in the artificed dramatic story of "The Mayor of Casterbridge"—and we cite this novel as characteristic, both in its strength and weakness, of its distinguished author,—that we are brought to feel that we have not been shown the characters of Casterbridge going their way in life naturally, but that they have been moved about, kaleidoscopically, to suit the exigencies of the plot, and that the more this is so the less significance for us have their thoughts and actions. Watching the quick whirling changes of Farfrae and Lucetta, Henchard and Newson in the matrimonial mazes of the story, and listening to the chorus of the rustics in the wings, we perceive indeed whence comes that atmosphere of stage crisis and stage effect which suddenly introduces a disillusioning sense of unreality, and mars the artistic unity of this charming picture, so truthful in other respects to English rural life. Plot is Mr. Hardy's weakness, and perfect indeed and convincing would have been his pictures, if he could have thrown his plots and his rustic choruses to the four winds. May we not be thankful, therefore, that Jefferies was no hand at elaborating a plot, and that in "Amaryllis at the Fair," the scenes, the descriptions, the conversations are spontaneous as life, and that Jefferies' commentary on them is like Fielding's commentary, a medium by which he lives with his characters. The author's imagination, memory, and instinctive perception are, indeed, all working together; and so his picture of human life in "Amaryllis" brings with it as convincing and as fresh a breath of life as we find in Cobbett's, Waugh's and Barnes' country writings. When a writer arrives at being perfectly natural in his atmosphere, his style and his subject seem to become one. He moves easily and surely. Out of the splintered mass of ideas and emotions, out of the sensations, the observations and revelations of his youth, and the atmosphere familiar to him through long feeling, he builds up a subtle and cunning picture for us, a complete illusion of life more true than the reality. For what prosaic people call the reality is merely the co-ordination in their own minds of perhaps a thousandth part of aspects of the life around them; and only this thousandth part they have noticed. But the creative mind builds up a living picture out of the thousands of aspects most of us are congenitally blind to. This is what Jefferies has done in "Amaryllis at the Fair." The book is rich in the contradictory forces of life, in its quick twists and turns: we feel in it there is nature working alike in the leaves of grass outside the Idens' house, in the blustering winds round the walls, and in the minds of the characters indoors; and the style has the freshness of the April wind. Everything is growing, changing, breathing in the book. But the accomplished critics do not notice these trivial strengths. It is enough for them that Jefferies was not a novelist! Indeed, Mr. Saintsbury apparently thinks that Jefferies made a mistake in drawing his philosophy from an open-air study of nature, for he writes: "Unfortunately for Jefferies his philosophic background was not like Wordsworth's clear and cheerful, but wholly vague and partly gloomy." It was neither vague nor gloomy, we may remark, parenthetically, but we may admit that Jefferies saw too deeply into nature's workings, and had too sensuous a joy in life to interpret all Nature's doings, à la Wordsworth, and lend them a portentously moral significance.

The one charge that may with truth be brought against "Amaryllis at the Fair" is that its digressions damage the artistic illusion of the whole. The book shows the carelessness, the haste, the roughness of a sketch, a sketch, moreover, which Jefferies was not destined to carry to the end he had planned, but we repeat, let us be thankful that its artistic weaknesses are those of a sketch direct from nature, rather than those of an ambitious studio picture. And these digressions are an integral part of the book's character, just as the face of a man has its own blemishes: they are one with the spirit of the whole, and so, if they break somewhat the illusion of the scenes, they do not damage its spiritual unity. It is this spiritual unity on which we must insist, because "Amaryllis" is indeed Jefferies' last and complete testament on human life. He wrote it, or rather dictated it to his wife, as he lay in pain, slowly dying, and he has put into it the frankness of a dying man. How real, how solid, how deliciously sweet seemed those simple earthly joys, those human appetites of healthy, vigorous men to him! how intense is his passion and spiritual hunger for the beauty of earth! Like a flame shooting up from the log it is consuming, so this passion for the green earth, for the earth in wind and rain and sunshine, consumes the wasted, consumptive body of the dying man. The reality, the solidity of the homely farmhouse life he describes spring from the intensity with which he clings to all he loves, the cold March wind buffeting the face, the mating cries of the birds in the hot spring sunshine. Life is so terribly strong, so deliciously real, so full of man's unsatisfied hungry ache for happiness; and sweet is the craving, bitter the knowledge of the unfulfilment. So, inspiring and vivifying the whole, in every line of "Amaryllis" is Jefferies' philosophy of life. Jefferies "did not understand human nature," say the accomplished critics. Did he not? "Amaryllis at the Fair" is one of the truest criticisms of human life, oh reader, you are likely to meet with. The mixedness of things, the old, old human muddle, the meanness and stupidity and shortsightedness of humanity, the good salty taste of life in the healthy mouth, the spirituality of love, the strong earthy roots of appetite, man's lust of life, with circumstances awry, and the sharp wind blowing alike on the just and the unjust— all is there on the printed page of "Amaryllis at the Fair." The song of the wind and the roar of London unite and mingle therein for those who do not bring the exacting eye of superiority to this most human book.

Edward Garnett

CHAPTER I

AMARYLLIS found the first daffodil flowering by the damask rose, and immediately ran to call her father to come and see it.

There are no damask roses now, like there used to be in summer at Coombe Oaks. I have never seen one since I last gathered one from that very bush. There are many grand roses, but no fragrance—the fragrance is gone out of life. Instinctively as I pass gardens in summer I look under the shade of the trees for the old roses, but they are not to be found. The dreary nurseries of evergreens and laurels—cemeteries they should be called, cemeteries in appearance and cemeteries of taste—are innocent of such roses. They show you an acre of what they call roses growing out of dirty straw, spindly things with a knob on the top, which even dew can hardly sweeten. "No call for damask roses—wouldn't pay to grow they. Single they was, I thinks. No good. These be cut every morning and fetched by the flower-girls for gents' button-holes and ladies' jackets. You won't get no damask roses; they be died out."

I think in despite of the nurseryman, or cemetery-keeper, that with patience I could get a damask rose even now by inquiring about from farmhouse to farmhouse. In time some old farmer, with a good old taste for old roses and pinks, would send me one; I have half a mind to try. But, alas! it is no use, I have nowhere to put it; I rent a house which is built in first-rate modern style, though small, of course, and there is a "garden" to it, but no place to put a damask rose. No place, because it is not "home," and I cannot plant except round "home." The plot or "patch" the landlord calls "the garden"—it is about as wide as the border round a patch, old style—is quite vacant, bare, and contains nothing but mould. It is nothing to me, and I cannot plant it.

Not only are there no damask roses, but there is no place for them now-a-days, no "home," only villas and rented houses. Anything rented in a town can never be "home."

Farms that were practically taken on a hundred and twenty, or fifty, or perhaps two hundred years' leases were "homes." Consequently they had damask roses, bees, and birds about them.

There had been daffodils in that spot at least a century, opening every March to the dry winds that shrivel up the brown dead leaves of winter, and carry them out from the bushes under the trees, sending them across the meadow—fleeing like a routed army

1

before the bayonets of the East. Every spring for a century at least the daffodils had bloomed there.

Amaryllis did not stay to think of the century, but ran round the corner of the house, and came face to face with the east wind, which took her with such force as to momentarily stay her progress. Her skirts were blown out horizontally, her ankles were exposed, and the front line of her shape (beginning to bud like spring) was sketched against the red brick wall. She laughed, but the strong gale filled her throat as if a hand had been thrust down it; the wind got its edge like a knife under her eyelids, between them and the eyeballs, and seemed as if it would scoop them out; her eyes were wet with involuntary tears; her lips dried up and parched in a moment. The wind went through her thick stockings as if the wool was nothing. She lifted her hand to defend her eyes, and the skin of her arm became "goosey" directly. Had she worn hat or bonnet it would have flown. Stooping forwards, she pushed step by step, and gradually reached the shelter of the high garden wall; there she could stand upright, and breathe again.

Her lips, which had been whitened by the keen blast, as if a storm of ice particles had been driven against them, now resumed their scarlet, but her ears were full of dust and reddened, and her curly dark hair was dry and rough and without gloss. Each separate hair separated itself from the next, and would not lie smooth—the natural unctuous essence which usually caused them to adhere was dried up.

The wind had blown thus round that corner every March for a century, and in no degree abated its bitter force because a beautiful human child, full of the happiness of a flower, came carelessly into its power. Nothing ever shows the least consideration for human creatures.

The moss on the ridge of the wall under which she stood to breathe looked shrivelled and thin, the green tint dried out of it. A sparrow with a straw tried hard to reach the eaves of the house to put it in his nest, but the depending straw was caught by the breeze as a sail, and carried him past.

Under the wall was a large patch recently dug, beside the patch a grass path, and on the path a wheelbarrow. A man was busy putting in potatoes; he wore the raggedest coat ever seen on a respectable back. As the wind lifted the tails it was apparent that the lining was loose and only hung by threads, the cuffs were worn through, there was a hole beneath each arm, and on each shoulder the nap of the cloth was gone; the colour, which had once been grey, was now a mixture of several soils and numerous kinds of grit. The hat he had on was no better; it might have been made of some hard

2

pasteboard, it was so bare. Every now and then the wind brought a few handfuls of dust over the wall from the road, and dropped it on his stooping back.

The way in which he was planting potatoes was wonderful, every potato was placed at exactly the right distance apart, and a hole made for it in the general trench; before it was set it was looked at and turned over, and the thumb rubbed against it to be sure that it was sound, and when finally put in, a little mould was delicately adjusted round to keep it in its right position till the whole row was buried. He carried the potatoes in his coat pocket—those, that is, for the row—and took them out one by one; had he been planting his own children he could not have been more careful. The science, the skill, and the experience brought to this potato-planting you would hardly credit; for all this care was founded upon observation, and arose from very large abilities on the part of the planter, though directed to so humble a purpose at that moment.

So soon as Amaryllis had recovered breath, she ran down the grass path and stood by the wheelbarrow, but although her shadow fell across the potato row, he would not see her.

"Pa," she said, not very loud. "Pa," growing bolder. "Do come—there's a daffodil out, the very, very first."

"Oh," a sound like a growl—"oh," from the depth of a vast chest heaving out a doubtful note.

"It is such a beautiful colour!"

"Where is your mother?" looking at her askance and still stooping.

"Indoors—at least—I think—no——"

"Haven't you got no sewing? Can't you help her? What good be you on?"

"But this is such a lovely daffodil, and the very first—now do come!"

"Flowers bean't no use on; such trumpery as that; what do'ee want a-messing about arter thaay? You'll never be no good on; you ain't never got a apron on."

"But—just a minute now."

"Go on in, and be some use on."

Amaryllis' lip fell; she turned and walked slowly away along the path, her head drooping forward.

Did ever anyone have a beautiful idea or feeling without being repulsed?

She had not reached the end of the path, however, when the father began to change his attitude; he stood up, dropped his "dibbler," scraped his foot on his spade, and, grumbling to himself, went after her. She did not see or hear him till he overtook her.

"Please, I'll go and do the sewing," she said.

"Where be this yer flower?" gruffly.

"I'll show you," taking his ragged arm, and brightening up immediately. "Only think, to open in all this wind, and so cold—isn't it beautiful? It's much more beautiful than the flowers that come in the summer."

"Trumpery rubbish—mean to dig 'em all up—would if I had time," muttered the father. "Have 'em carted out and drowed away—do for ashes to drow on the fields. Never no good on to nobody, thaay thengs. You can't eat 'em, can you, like you can potatoes?"

"But it's lovely. Here it is," and Amaryllis stepped on the patch tenderly, and lifted up the drooping face of the flower.

"Ah, yes," said Iden, putting his left hand to his chin, a habit of his when thinking, and suddenly quite altering his pronunciation from that of the country folk and labourers amongst whom he dwelt to the correct accent of education. "Ah, yes; the daffodil was your great-uncle's favourite flower."

"Richard?" asked Amaryllis.

"Richard," repeated Iden. And Amaryllis, noting how handsome her father's intellectual face looked, wandered in her mind from the flower as he talked, and marvelled how he could be so rough sometimes, and why he talked like the labourers, and wore a ragged coat—he who was so full of wisdom in his other moods, and spoke, and thought, and indeed acted as a perfect gentleman.

"Richard's favourite flower," he went on. "He brought the daffodils down from Luckett's; every one in the garden came from there. He was always reading poetry, and writing, and sketching, and yet he was such a capital man of business; no one could understand that. He built the mill, and saved heaps of money; he bought back the old place at Luckett's, which belonged to us before Queen Elizabeth's days; indeed, he very nearly made up the fortunes Nicholas and the rest of them got rid of. He was, indeed, a man. And now it is all going again—faster than he made it. He used to take you on his knee and say you would walk well, because you had a good ankle."

Amaryllis blushed and smoothed her dress with her hands, as if that would lengthen the skirt and hide the ankles which Richard, the great-uncle, had admired when she was a child, being a man, but which her feminine acquaintances told her were heavy.

"Here, put on your hat and scarf; how foolish of you to go out in this wind without them!" said Mrs. Iden, coming out. She thrust them into Amaryllis' unwilling hands, and retired indoors again immediately.

4

"He was the only one of all the family," continued her father, "who could make money; all the rest could do nothing but spend it. For ten generations he was the only money-maker and saver, and yet he was as free and liberal as possible. Very curious, wasn't it?— only one in ten generations—difficult to understand why none of the others—why——" He paused, thinking.

Amaryllis, too, was silent, thinking—thinking how easily her papa could make money, great heaps of money. She was sure he could if he tried, instead of planting potatoes.

"If only another Richard would rise up like him!" said Iden.

This was a very unreasonable wish, for, having had one genius in the family, and that, too, in the memory of man, they could not expect another. Even vast empires rarely produce more than one great man in all the course of their history. There was but one Cæsar in the thousand years of Rome; Greece never had one as a nation, unless we except Themistocles, or unless we accept Alexander, who was a Macedonian; Persia had a Cyrus; there was a Tamerlane somewhere, but few people know anything of the empire he overshadows with his name; France has had two mighty warriors, Charlemagne and Napoleon—unfortunate France! As for ourselves, fortunate islanders! we have never had a great man so immensely great as to overtop the whole, like Charlemagne in his day. Fortunate for us, indeed, that it has been so. But the best example to the point is the case of the immense empire of Russia, which has had one Peter the Great, and one only. Great-uncle Richard was the Peter the Great of his family, whose work had been slowly undone by his successors.

"I wonder whether any of us will ever turn out like Richard," continued Iden. "No one could deny him long; he had a way of persuading and convincing people, and always got his own will in the end. Wonderful man!" he pondered, returning towards his work.

Suddenly the side door opened, and Mrs. Iden just peered out, and cried, "Put your hat and scarf on directly."

Amaryllis put the hat on, and wound the scarf very loosely about her neck. She accompanied her father to the potato patch, hoping that he would go on talking, but he was quickly absorbed in the potatoes. She watched him stooping till his back was an arch; in fact, he had stooped so much that now he could not stand upright, though still in the prime of life; if he stood up and stretched himself, still his back was bowed at the shoulders. He worked so hard—ever since she could remember she had seen him working like this; he was up in the morning while it was yet dark tending the cattle; sometimes he was up all night with them, wind or weather made no difference. Other people stopped indoors if it rained much, but it made no difference to her father, nor did the deep snow or the sharp frosts. Always at work, and he could talk so cleverly, too, and knew everything, and yet they were so short of money. How could this be?

What a fallacy it is that hard work is the making of money; I could show you plenty of men who have worked the whole of their lives as hard as ever could possibly be, and who are still as far off independence as when they began. In fact, that is the rule; the winning of independence is rarely the result of work, else nine out of ten would be well-to-do.

CHAPTER II

PRESENTLY Amaryllis wandered indoors, and was met in the hall by her mother.

"What has he been talking to you about?" she said, angrily. "Don't listen to him. He will never do any good. Just look at his coat; it's a disgrace, a positive disgrace. Telling you about the old people? What's the use of talking of people who have been dead all this time? Why doesn't he do something himself? Don't listen to his rubbish—wasting his time there with potatoes, it is enough to make one wild! Why doesn't he go in to market and buy and sell cattle, and turn over money in that way? Not he! he'd rather muddle with a few paltry potatoes, as if it mattered an atom how they were stuck in the ground."

Not liking to hear her father abused, Amaryllis went upstairs, and when she was alone lifted her skirt and looked at the ankles which great-uncle Richard had admired. Other girls had told her they were thick, and she was ashamed of them.

Instead of the slender things which seem as if a sudden strain would snap them, and are nothing but mere bone, she had a pair of well-shaped ankles, justly proportioned to what would soon be a fine form; strong, but neither thick, nor coarse, nor heavy, ankles that would carry her many a mile without weariness, that ended good legs with plenty of flesh on them. The stupidity of calling such coarse or heavy! They were really ideal ankles, such as a sculptor would carve. Yet these ill-instructed girls called them coarse! It was

6

not their fault, it was the lack of instruction; as they did not know what was physically perfect, of course they could not recognize it.

Let every girl who has such ankles be proud of them, for they will prove a blessing to her for the whole of her life.

Amaryllis could not get her hair smooth, though she brushed it for some time; it would not lie close, so much had the east wind dried it. She opened a drawer, and took out a little bottle of macassar, and held it in her hand, balancing probabilities. Would her father see it if she used it, or might he, perhaps, fail to notice? She dared not leave the bottle on the dressing-table, for if he had chanced to pass through the room he would certainly have thrown it out of window, so bitter was his antagonism to all oils and perfumes, scents, pomades, and other resources of the hairdresser, which he held defiled the hair and ruined it, to the deception of woman and the disgust of man. Not one drop of scent did Amaryllis dare to sprinkle on her handkerchief, not one drop of oil did she dare put on her beautiful hair unless surreptitiously, and then she could not go near him, for he was certain to detect it and scorch her with withering satire.

Yet, however satirized, feminine faith in perfumes and oils and so forth is like a perennial spring, and never fails.

Such splendid hair as Amaryllis possessed needed no dressing—nothing could possibly improve it, and the chances therefore were that whatever she used would injure—yet in her heart she yearned to rub it with oil.

But the more she considered the more probable it seemed that her father would detect her; she had better wait till he went out for the afternoon somewhere, an event that seldom occurred, for Iden was one of those who preferred working at home to rambling abroad. He was, indeed, too attached to his home work. So she returned the bottle to the drawer, and hid it under some stockings.

Immediately afterwards it was dinner-time. At all meals the rule was that there must be no talking, but at dinner the law was so strict that even to ask for anything, as a piece of bread, or to say so much as "Give me the salt, please," was a deadly sin. There must be absolute silence while the master ate. The least infringement was visited with a severe glance from his keen and brilliant blue eyes— there are no eyes so stern as blue eyes when angry—or else he uttered a deep sigh like a grunt, and sat rigidly upright for a moment. For he usually stooped, and to sit upright showed annoyance. No laws of the Medes and Persians were ever obeyed as was this law of silence in that house.

Anything that disturbed the absolute calm of the dinner hour was worse than sacrilege; anything that threatened to disturb it was watched intently by that repressive eye. No one must come in or go out of the room; if anyone knocked at the door (there are no bells in old country houses) there was a frown immediately, it necessitated someone answering it, and then Mrs. Iden or Amaryllis had to leave the table, to go out and open and shut the sitting-room door as they went, and again as they returned. Amaryllis dreaded a knock at the door, it was so awful to have to stir once they had sat down to dinner, and the servant was certain not to know what reply to give. Sometimes it happened—and this was very terrible—that the master himself had to go, some one wanted him about some hay or a horse and cart, and no one could tell what to do but the master. A dinner broken up in this way was a very serious matter indeed.

That day they had a leg of mutton—a special occasion—a joint to be looked on reverently. Mr. Iden had walked into the town to choose it himself some days previously, and brought it home on foot in a flag basket. The butcher would have sent it, and if not, there were men on the farm who could have fetched it, but it was much too important to be left to a second person. No one could do it right but Mr. Iden himself. There was a good deal of reason in this personal care of the meat, for it is a certain fact that unless you do look after such things yourself, and that persistently, too, you never get it first-rate. For this cause people in grand villas scarcely ever have anything worth eating on their tables. Their household expenses reach thousands yearly, and yet they rarely have anything eatable, and their dinner-tables can never show meat, vegetables, or fruit equal to Mr. Iden's. The meat was dark brown, as mutton should be, for if it is the least bit white it is sure to be poor; the grain was short, and ate like bread and butter, firm, and yet almost crumbling to the touch; it was full of juicy red gravy, and cut pleasantly, the knife went through it nicely; you can tell good meat directly you touch it with the knife. It was cooked to a turn, and had been done at a wood fire on a hearth; no oven taste, no taint of coal gas or carbon; the pure flame of wood had browned it. Such emanations as there may be from burning logs are odorous of the woodland, of the sunshine, of the fields and fresh air; the wood simply gives out as it burns the sweetness it has imbibed through its leaves from the atmosphere which floats above grass and flowers. Essences of this order, if they do penetrate the fibres of the meat, add to its flavour a delicate aroma. Grass-fed meat, cooked at a wood fire, for me.

Wonderful it is that wealthy people can endure to have their meat cooked over coal or in a shut-up iron box, where it kills itself with its own steam, which ought to escape. But then wealthy villa people do do odd things. Les Misérables who have to write like myself must put up with anything and be thankful for permission to exist; but people with mighty incomes from tea, or crockery-ware, or mud, or bricks and mortar—why on earth these happy and favoured mortals do not live like the gods passes understanding.

Parisian people use charcoal: perhaps Paris will convert some of you who will not listen to a farmer.

Mr. Iden had himself grown the potatoes that were placed before him. They were white, floury, without a drop of water in the whole dish of them. They were equal to the finest bread—far, far superior to the bread with which the immense city of London permits itself to be poisoned. (It is not much better, for it destroys the digestion.) This, too, with wheat at thirty shillings the quarter, a price which is in itself one of the most wonderful things of the age. The finest bread ought to be cheap.

"They be forty-folds," said Mr. Iden, helping himself to half a dozen. "Look at the gravy go up into um like tea up a knob of sugar."

The gravy was drawn up among the dry, floury particles of the potatoes as if they had formed capillary tubes.

"Forty-folds," he repeated; "they comes forty to one. It be an amazing theng how thengs do that; forty grows for one. Thaay be an old-fashioned potato; you won't find many of thaay, not true forty-folds. Mine comes true, 'cause I saves um every year a' purpose. Better take more than that (to Amaryllis)—you haven't got but two" (to Mrs. Iden).

What he ate other people at his table must eat, and the largest quantity possible. No one else must speak, hardly to say "Yes" or "No," but the master could talk, talk, talk without end. The only talking that might be done by others was in praise of the edibles on the table by Iden so carefully provided. You might admire the potatoes or the mutton, but you must not talk on any other subject. Nor was it safe even to do that, because if you said, "What capital potatoes!" you were immediately helped to another plateful, and had to finish them, want them or not. If you praised the mutton several thick slices were placed on your plate, and woe to you if you left a particle. It was no use to try and cover over what you could not manage with knife and fork; it was sure to be seen. "What bean't you going to yet (eat) up that there juicy bit, you?"

Amaryllis and Mrs. Iden, warned by previous experience, discreetly refrained from admiring either mutton or potatoes.

CHAPTER III

FORTY-FOLDS," went on the master, "be the best keeping potatoes. Thur be so many new sorts now, but they bean't no good; they be very good for gentlefolk as doan't know no better, and poor folk as can't help theirselves. They won't grow everywhere neither; there bean't but one patch in our garden as ull grow 'um well. It's that's big middle patch. Summat different in the soil thur. There's a lot, bless you! to be learned before you can grow a potato, for all it looks such a simple thing. Farty-folds——"

"Farty-folds!" said Mrs. Iden, imitating his provincial pronunciation with extreme disgust in her tone.

"Aw, yes, too," said Iden. "Varty-volds be ould potatoes, and thur bean't none as can beat um."

The more she showed her irritation at his speech or ways, the more he accentuated both language and manner.

"Talking with your mouth full," said Mrs. Iden. It was true, Iden did talk with his mouth full, very full indeed, for he fed heartily. The remark annoyed him; he grunted and spluttered and choked a little—floury things are choky. He got it down by taking a long draught at his quart of strong ale. Splendid ale it was, too, the stuff to induce you to make faces at Goliath. He soon began to talk again.

"Th' ould shepherd fetched me these swede greens; I axed un three days ago; I know'd we was going to have this yer mutton. You got to settle these yer things aforehand."

"Axed," muttered Mrs. Iden.

"Th' pigeons have been at um, they be 'mazing fond of um, so be the larks. These be the best as thur was. They be the best things in the world for the blood. Swede greens be the top of all physic. If you can get fresh swede tops you don't want a doctor within twenty miles. Their's nothing in all the chemists' shops in England equal to swede greens"—helping himself to a large quantity of salt.

"What a lot of salt you do eat!" muttered Mrs. Iden.

"Onely you must have the real swedes—not thuck stuff they sells in towns; greens they was once p'rhaps, but they be tough as leather, and haven't got a drop of sap in um. Swedes is onely to be got about March."

"Pooh! you can get them at Christmas in London," said Mrs. Iden.

"Aw, can 'ee? Call they swede tops? They bean't no good; you

10

might as well eat dried leaves. I tell you these are the young fresh green shoots of spring"—suddenly changing his pronunciation as he became interested in his subject and forgot the shafts of irritation shot at him by his wife. "They are full of sap—fresh sap—the juice which the plant extracts from the earth as the active power of the sun's rays increases. It is this sap which is so good for the blood. Without it the vegetable is no more than a woody fibre. Why the sap should be so powerful I cannot tell you; no one knows, any more than they know how the plant prepares it. This is one of those things which defy analysis—the laboratory is at fault, and can do nothing with it." ("More salt!" muttered Mrs. Iden. "How can you eat such a quantity of salt?") "There is something beyond what the laboratory can lay hands on; something that cannot be weighed, or seen, or estimated, neither by quantity, quality, or by any means. They analyse champagne, for instance; they find so many parts water, so much sugar, so much this, and so much that; but out of the hundred parts there remain ten—I think it is ten—at all events so many parts still to be accounted for. They escape, they are set down as volatile—the laboratory has not even a distinct name for this component; the laboratory knows nothing at all about it, cannot even name it. But this unknown constituent is the real champagne. So it is with the sap. In spring the sap possesses a certain virtue; at other times of the year the leaf is still green, but useless to us."

"I shall have some vinegar," said Mrs. Iden, defiantly, stretching out her hand to the cruet.

Mr. Iden made a wry face, as if the mere mention of vinegar had set his teeth on edge. He looked the other way and ate as fast as he could, to close his eyes to the spectacle of any one spoiling the sappy swede greens with nauseous vinegar. To his system of edible philosophy vinegar was utterly antagonistic—destructive of the sap-principle, altogether wrong, and, in fact, wicked, as destroying good and precious food.

Amaryllis would not have dared to have taken the vinegar herself, but as her mother passed the cruet to her, she, too, fell away, and mixed vinegar with the green vegetables. All women like vinegar.

When the bottle was restored to the cruet-stand Mr. Iden deigned to look round again at the table.

"Ha! you'll cut your thumb!" he shouted to Amaryllis, who was cutting a piece of bread. She put the loaf down with a consciousness of guilt. "Haven't I told you how to cut bread twenty times? Cutting towards your thumb like that! Hold your left hand lower down, so that if the knife slips it will go over. Here, like this. Give it to me."

11

He cut a slice to show her, and then tossed the slice across the table so accurately that it fell exactly into its proper place by her plate. He had a habit of tossing things in that way.

"Why ever couldn't you pass it on the tray?" said Mrs. Iden. "Flinging in that manner! I hate to see it."

Amaryllis, as in duty bound, in appearance took the lesson in bread-cutting to heart, as she had done twenty times before. But she knew she should still cut a loaf in the same dangerous style when out of his sight. She could not do it in the safe way—it was so much easier in the other; and if she did cut her hand she did not greatly care.

"Now perhaps you'll remember," said the master, getting up with his plate in his hand.

"Whatever are you going to do now?" asked Mrs. Iden, who knew perfectly well.

"Going to warm the plate." He went out into the kitchen, sat down by the fire, and carefully warmed his plate for a second helping.

"I should think you couldn't want any more," said Mrs. Iden when he came back. "You had enough the first time for three."

But Iden, who had the appetite of a giant, and had never ruined his digestion with vinegar or sauces, piled another series of thick slices on his plate, now hot to liquefy the gravy, and added to the meat a just proportion of vegetables. In proportion and a just mixture the secret of eating successfully consisted, according to him.

First he ate a piece of the dark brown mutton, this was immediately followed by a portion of floury potato, next by a portion of swede tops, and then, lest a too savoury taste should remain in the mouth, he took a fragment of bread, as it were to sweeten and cleanse his teeth. Finally came a draught of strong ale, and after a brief moment the same ingredients were mixed in the same order as before. His dinner was thus eaten in a certain order, and with a kind of rhythm, duly exciting each particular flavour like a rhyme in its proper position, and duly putting it out with its correct successor. Always the savour of meat and gravy and vegetables had to be toned down by the ultimate bread, a vast piece of which he kept beside him. He was a great bread eater—it was always bread after everything, and if there were two courses then bread between to prepare the palate, and to prevent the sweets from quarrelling with the acids. Organization was the chief characteristic of his mind—his very dinner was organized and well planned, and any break or disturbance was not so much an annoyance in itself as

12

destructive of a clever design, like a stick thrust through the web of a geometrical spider.

This order of mouthfuls had been explained over and over again to the family, and if they felt that he was in a more than usually terrible mood, and if they felt his gaze upon them, the family to some extent submitted. Neither Mrs. Iden nor Amaryllis, however, could ever educate their palates into this fixed sequence of feeding; and, if Iden was not in a very awful and Jovelike mood, they wandered about irregularly in their eating. When the dinner was over (and, indeed, before it began) they had a way of visiting the larder, and "picking" little fragments of pies, or cold fowl, even a cold potato, the smallest mug—a quarter of a pint of the Goliath ale between them, or, if it was to be had, a sip of port wine. These women were very irrational in their feeding; they actually put vinegar on cold cabbage; they gloated over a fragment of pickled salmon about eleven o'clock in the morning. They had a herring sometimes for tea—the smell of it cooking sent the master into fits of indignation, he abominated it so, but they were so hardened and lost to righteousness they always repeated the offence next time the itinerant fish-dealer called. You could not drum them into good solid, straightforward eating.

They generally had a smuggled bit of pastry to eat in the kitchen after dinner, for Mr. Iden considered that no one could need a second course after first-rate mutton and forty-folds. A morsel of cheese if you liked—nothing more. In summer the great garden abounded with fruit; he would have nothing but rhubarb, rhubarb, rhubarb, day after day, or else black-currant pudding. He held that black currants were the most wholesome fruit that grew; if he fancied his hands were not quite clean he would rub them with black-currant leaves to give them a pleasant aromatic odour (as ladies use scented soap). He rubbed them with walnut-leaves for the same purpose.

Of salad in its season he was a great eater, cucumber especially, and lettuce and celery; but a mixed salad (oil and a flash, as it were, of Worcester sauce) was a horror to him. A principle ran through all his eating—an idea, a plan and design.

I assure you it is a very important matter this eating, a man's fortune depends on his dinner. I should have been as rich as Crœsus if I could only have eaten what I liked all my time; I am sure I should, now I come to look back.

The soundest and most wholesome food in the world was set on Mr. Iden's table; you may differ from his system, but you would have enjoyed the dark brown mutton, the floury potatoes, the fresh vegetables and fruit and salad, and the Goliath ale.

When he had at last finished his meal he took his knife and carefully scraped his crumbs together, drawing the edge along the cloth, first one way and then the other, till he had a little heap; for, eating so much bread, he made many crumbs. Having got them together, he proceeded to shovel them into his mouth with the end of his knife, so that not one was wasted. Sometimes he sprinkled a little moist sugar over them with his finger and thumb. He then cut himself a slice of bread and cheese, and sat down with it in his arm-chair by the fire, spreading his large red-and-yellow silk handkerchief on his knee to catch the fragments in lieu of a plate.

"Why can't you eat your cheese at the table, like other people?" said Mrs. Iden, shuffling her feet with contemptuous annoyance. A deep grunt in the throat was the answer she received; at the same time he turned his arm-chair more towards the fire, as much as to say, "Other people are nothing to me."

CHAPTER IV

THIS arm-chair, of old-fashioned make, had lost an arm—the screw remained sticking up, but the woodwork on that side was gone. It had been accidentally broken some ten years since; yet, although he used the chair every day, the arm had never been mended. Awkward as it was, he let it alone.

"Hum! where's The Standard, then?" he said presently, as he nibbled his cheese and sipped the ale which he had placed on the hob.

"Here it is, Pa," said Amaryllis, hastening with the paper.

"Thought you despised the papers?" said Mrs. Iden. "Thought there was nothing but lies and rubbish in them, according to you?"

"No more thur bean't."

"You always take good care to read them, though."

"Hum!" Another deep grunt, and another slight turn of the chair. He could not answer this charge of inconsistency, for it was a fact that he affected to despise the newspaper and yet read it with avidity, and would almost as soon have missed his ale as his news.

However, to settle with his conscience, he had a manner of holding the paper half aslant a good way from him, and every now and then as he read uttered a dissentient or disgusted grunt.

The master's taking up his paper was a signal for all other persons to leave the room, and not to return till he had finished his news and his nap.

Mrs. Iden and Amaryllis, as they went out, each took as many of the dishes as they could carry, for it was uncertain when they could come in again to clear the table. The cloth must not be moved, the door opened, or the slightest sound heard till the siesta was over.

"Can't clear the dinner things till four o'clock," said Mrs. Iden as she went, "and then you want your tea—senseless!" Amaryllis shut the door, and the master was left to himself.

By-and-by, his cheese being finished, he dropped his newspaper, and arranged himself for slumber. His left elbow he carefully fitted to the remnant of the broken woodwork of the chair. The silk handkerchief, red and yellow, he gathered into a loose pad in his left hand for his cheek and temple to rest on. His face was thus supported by his hand and arm, while the side of his head touched and rested against the wainscot of the wall.

Just where his head touched it the wainscot had been worn away by the daily pressure, leaving a round spot. The wood was there exposed—a round spot, an inch or two in diameter, being completely bare of varnish. So many nods—the attrition of thirty years and more of nodding—had gradually ground away the coat with which the painter had originally covered the wood. It even looked a little hollow—a little depressed—as if his head had scooped out a shallow crater; but this was probably an illusion, the eye being deceived by the difference in colour between the wood and the varnish around it.

This human mark reminded one of the grooves worn by the knees of generations of worshippers in the sacred steps of the temple which they ascended on all-fours. It was, indeed, a mark of devotion, as Mrs. Iden and others, not very keen observers, would have said, to the god of Sleep; in truth, it was a singular instance of continued devotion at the throne of the god of Thought.

It was to think that Mr. Iden in the commencement assumed this posture of slumber, and commanded silence. But thought which has been cultivated for a third of a century is apt to tone down to something very near somnolence.

That panel of wainscot was, in fact, as worthy of preservation as those on which the early artists delineated the Madonna and Infant, and for which high prices are now paid. It was intensely—superlatively—human. Worn in slow time by a human head within which a great mind was working under the most unhappy

15

conditions, it had the deep value attaching to inanimate things which have witnessed intolerable suffering.

I am not a Roman Catholic, but I must confess that if I could be assured any particular piece of wood had really formed a part of the Cross I should think it the most valuable thing in the world, to which Koh-i-noors would be mud.

I am a pagan, and think the heart and soul above crowns.

That panel was in effect a cross on which a heart had been tortured for the third of a century, that is, for the space of time allotted to a generation.

That mark upon the panel had still a further meaning, it represented the unhappiness, the misfortunes, the Nemesis of two hundred years. This family of Idens had endured already two hundred years of unhappiness and discordance for no original fault of theirs, simply because they had once been fortunate of old time, and therefore they had to work out that hour of sunshine to the utmost depths of shadow.

The panel of the wainscot upon which that mark had been worn was in effect a cross upon which a human heart had been tortured—and thought can, indeed, torture—for a third of a century. For Iden had learned to know himself, and despaired.

Not long after he had settled himself and closed his eyes the handle of the door was very softly turned, and Amaryllis stole in for her book, which she had forgotten. She succeeded in getting it on tiptoe without a sound, but in shutting the door the lock clicked, and she heard him kick the fender angrily with his iron-shod heel.

After that there was utter silence, except the ticking of the American clock—a loud and distinct tick in the still (and in that sense vacant) room.

Presently a shadow somewhat darkened the window, a noiseless shadow; Mrs. Iden had come quietly round the house, and stood in the March wind, watching the sleeping man. She had a shawl about her shoulders—she put out her clenched hand from under its folds, and shook her fist at him, muttering to herself, "Never do anything; nothing but sleep, sleep, sleep: talk, talk, talk; never do anything. That's what I hate."

The noiseless shadow disappeared; the common American clock continued its loud tick, tick.

Slight sounds, faint rustlings, began to be audible among the cinders in the fender. The dry cinders were pushed about by something passing between them. After a while a brown mouse peered out at the end of the fender under Iden's chair, looked round a moment, and went back to the grate. In a minute he came again, and ventured somewhat farther across the width of the white

16

hearthstone to the verge of the carpet. This advance was made step by step, but on reaching the carpet the mouse rushed home to cover in one run—like children at "touch wood," going out from a place of safety very cautiously, returning swiftly. The next time another mouse followed, and a third appeared at the other end of the fender. By degrees they got under the table, and helped themselves to the crumbs; one mounted a chair and reached the cloth, but soon descended, afraid to stay there. Five or six mice were now busy at their dinner.

The sleeping man was as still and quiet as if carved.

A mouse came to the foot, clad in a great rusty-hued iron-shod boot—the foot that rested on the fender, for he had crossed his knees. His ragged and dingy trouser, full of March dust, and earth-stained by labour, was drawn up somewhat higher than the boot. It took the mouse several trials to reach the trouser, but he succeeded, and audaciously mounted to Iden's knee. Another quickly followed, and there the pair of them feasted on the crumbs of bread and cheese caught in the folds of his trousers.

One great brown hand was in his pocket, close to them—a mighty hand, beside which they were pigmies indeed in the land of the giants. What would have been the value of their lives between a finger and thumb that could crack a ripe and strong-shelled walnut?

The size—the mass—the weight of his hand alone was as a hill overshadowing them; his broad frame like the Alps; his head high above as a vast rock that overhung the valley.

His thumb-nail—widened by labour with spade and axe—his thumb-nail would have covered either of the tiny creatures as his shield covered Ajax.

Yet the little things fed in perfect confidence. He was so still, so very still—quiescent—they feared him no more than they did the wall; they could not hear his breathing.

Had they been gifted with human intelligence that very fact would have excited their suspicions. Why so very, very still? Strong men, wearied by work, do not sleep quietly; they breathe heavily. Even in firm sleep we move a little now and then, a limb trembles, a muscle quivers, or stretches itself.

But Iden was so still it was evident he was really wide awake and restraining his breath, and exercising conscious command over his muscles, that this scene might proceed undisturbed.

Now the strangeness of the thing was in this way: Iden set traps for mice in the cellar and the larder, and slew them there without mercy. He picked up the trap, swung it round, opening the door at the same instant, and the wretched captive was dashed to

17

death upon the stone flags of the floor. So he hated them and persecuted them in one place, and fed them in another.

A long psychological discussion might be held on this apparent inconsistency, but I shall leave analysis to those who like it, and go on recording facts. I will only make one remark. That nothing is consistent that is human. If it was not inconsistent it would have no association with a living person.

From the merest thin slit, as it were, between his eyelids, Iden watched the mice feed and run about his knees till, having eaten every crumb, they descended his leg to the floor.

CHAPTER V

HE was not asleep—he was thinking. Sometimes, of course, it happened that slumber was induced by the position in which he placed himself; slumber, however, was not his intent. He liked to rest after his midday meal and think. There was no real loss of time in it—he had been at work since half-past five.

His especial and striking characteristic was a very large, high, and noble forehead—the forehead attributed to Shakespeare and seen in his busts. Shakespeare's intellect is beyond inquiry, yet he was not altogether a man of action. He was, indeed, an actor upon the stage; once he stole the red deer (delightful to think of that!), but he did not sail to the then new discovered lands of America, nor did he fight the Spaniards. So much intellect is, perhaps, antagonistic to action, or rather it is averse to those arts by which a soldier climbs to the position of commander. If Shakespeare by the chance of birth, or other accident, had had the order of England's forces, we should have seen generalship such as the world had not known since Cæsar.

His intellect was too big to climb backstairs till opportunity came. We have great thoughts instead of battles.

Iden's forehead might have been sculptured for Shakespeare's. There was too much thought in it for the circumstances of his life. It is possible to think till you cannot act.

After the mice descended Iden did sleep for a few minutes. When he awoke he looked at the clock in a guilty way, and then opening the oven of the grate, took out a baked apple. He had one there ready for him almost always—always, that is, when they were not ripe on the trees.

A baked apple, he said, was the most wholesome thing in the world; it corrected the stomach, prevented acidity, improved digestion, and gave tone to all the food that had been eaten previously. If people would only eat baked apples they would not need to be for ever going to the chemists' shops for drugs and salines to put them right. The women were always at the chemists' shops—you could never pass the chemists' shops in the town without seeing two or three women buying something.

The apple was the apple of fruit, the natural medicine of man—and the best flavoured. It was compounded of the sweetest extracts and essences of air and light, put together of sunshine and wind and shower in such a way that no laboratory could imitate: and so on in a strain and with a simplicity of language that reminded you of Bacon and his philosophy of the Elizabethan age.

Iden in a way certainly had a tinge of the Baconian culture, naturally, and not from any study of that author, whose books he had never seen. The great Bacon was, in fact, a man of orchard and garden, and gathered his ideas from the fields.

Just look at an apple on the tree, said Iden. Look at a Blenheim orange, the inimitable mixture of colour, the gold and bronze, and ruddy tints, not bright colours—undertones of bright colours—smoothed together and polished, and made the more delightful by occasional roughness in the rind. Or look at the brilliant King Pippin. Now he was getting older he found, however, that the finest of them all was the russet. For eating, at its proper season, it was good, but for cooking it was simply the Imperial Cæsar and Sultan of apples; whether for baking, or pies, or sauce, there was none to equal it. Apple-sauce made of the real true russet was a sauce for Jove's own table. It was necessary that it should be the real russet. Indeed in apple trees you had to be as careful of breeding and pedigree as the owners of racing stables were about their horses.

Ripe apples could not be got all the year round in any variety; besides which, in winter and cold weather the crudity of the stomach needed to be assisted with a little warmth; therefore bake them.

People did not eat nearly enough fruit now-a-days; they had too much butcher's meat, and not enough fruit—that is, home-grown fruit, straight from orchard or garden, not the half-sour stuff sold in the shops, picked before it was ready.

The Americans were much wiser (he knew a good deal about

19

America—he had been there in his early days, before thought superseded action)—the Americans had kept up many of the fine old English customs of two or three hundred years since, and among these was the eating of fruit. They were accused of being so modern, so very, very modern, but, in fact, the country Americans, with whom he had lived (and who had taught him how to chop) maintained much of the genuine antique life of old England.

They had first-rate apples, yet it was curious that the same trees produced an apple having a slightly different flavour to what it had in this country. You could always distinguish an American apple by its peculiar piquancy—a sub-acid piquancy, a wild strawberry piquancy, a sort of woodland, forest, backwoods delicacy of its own. And so on, and so on—"talk, talk, talk," as Mrs. Iden said.

After his baked apple he took another guilty look at the clock, it was close on four, and went into the passage to get his hat. In farmhouses these places are called passages; in the smallest of villas, wretched little villas not fit to be called houses, they are always "halls."

In the passage Mrs. Iden was waiting for him, and began to thump his broad though bowed back with all her might.

"Sleep, sleep, sleep!" she cried, giving him a thump at each word. "You've slept two hours. (Thump.) You sleep till you stupefy yourself (thump), and then you go and dig. What's the use of digging? (Thump.) Why don't you make some money? (Thump.) Talk and sleep! (Thump.) I hate it. (Thump.) You've rubbed the paint off the wainscot with your sleep, sleep, sleep (thump)—there's one of your hairs sticking to the paint where your head goes. (Thump.) Anything more hateful—sleep (thump), talk (thump), sleep (thump). Go on!"

She had thumped him down the passage, and across the covered-in court to the door opening on the garden. There he paused to put on his hat—an aged, battered hat—some sort of nondescript bowler, broken, grey, weather-stained, very battered and very aged—a pitiful hat to put above that broad, Shakespearian forehead. While he fitted it on he was thumped severely: when he opened the door he paused, and involuntarily looked up at the sky to see about the weather—a habit all country people have—and so got more thumping, ending as he started out with a tremendous push. He did not seem to resent the knocks, nor did the push accelerate his pace; he took it very much as he took the March wind.

Mrs. Iden slammed the door, and went in to clear the dinner things, and make ready for tea. Amaryllis helped her.

"He'll want his tea in half an hour," said Mrs. Iden. "What's the use of his going out to work for half an hour?"

20

Amaryllis was silent. She was very fond of her father; he never did anything wrong in her eyes, and she could have pointed out that when he sat down to dinner at one he had already worked as many hours as Mrs. Iden's model City gentleman in a whole day. His dinner at one was, in effect, equivalent to their dinner at seven or eight, over which they frequently lingered an hour or two. He would still go on labouring, almost another half day. But she held her peace, for, on the other hand, she could not contradict and argue with her mother, whom she knew had had a wearisome life and perpetual disappointments.

Mrs. Iden grumbled on to herself, working herself into a more fiery passion, till at last she put down the tea-pot, and rushed into the garden. There as she came round the first thing she saw was the daffodil, the beautiful daffodil Amaryllis had discovered. Beside herself with indignation—what was the use of flowers or potatoes?—Mrs. Iden stepped on the border and trampled the flower under foot till it was shapeless. After this she rushed indoors again and upstairs to her bedroom, where she locked herself in, and fumbled about in the old black oak chest of drawers till she found a faded lavender glove.

That glove had been worn at the old "Ship" at Brighton years and years ago in the honeymoon trip: in those days bridal parties went down by coach. Faded with years, it had also faded from the tears that had fallen upon it. She turned it over in her hands, and her tears spotted it once more.

Amaryllis went on with the tea-making; for her mother to rush away in that manner was nothing new. She toasted her father a piece of toast—he affected to despise toast, but he always ate it if it was there, and looked about for it if it was not, though he never said anything. The clock struck five, and out she went to tell him tea was ready. Coming round the house she found her daffodil crushed to pieces.

"Oh!" The blood rushed to her forehead; then her beautiful lips pouted and quivered; tears filled her eyes, and her breast panted. She knew immediately who had done it; she ran to her bedroom to cry and to hide her grief and indignation.

CHAPTER VI

LADY-DAY Fair came round by and by, and Amaryllis, about eleven o'clock in the morning, went down the garden to the end of the orchard, where she could overlook the highway without being seen, and watch the folk go past. Just there the road began to descend into a hollow, while the garden continued level, so that Amaryllis, leaning her arm on the top of the wall, was much higher up than those who went along. The wall dropped quite fourteen feet down to the road, a rare red brick wall—thick and closely-built, the bricks close together with thin seams of mortar, so that the fibres of the whole mass were worked and compressed and bound firm, like the fibres of a piece of iron. The deep red bricks had a colour—a certain richness of stability—and at the top this good piece of workmanship was protected from the weather by a kind of cap, and ornamented with a projecting ridge. Within the wall Amaryllis could stand on a slight bank, and easily look over it. Without there was a sheer red precipice of fourteen feet down to the dusty sward and nettles beside the road.

Some bare branches of a plum tree trained against the wall rose thin and tapering above it in a bunch, a sign of bad gardening, for they ought to have been pruned, and the tree, indeed, had an appearance of neglect. One heavy bough had broken away from the nails and list, and drooped to the ground, and the shoots of last year, not having been trimmed, thrust themselves forward presumptuously.

Behind the bunch of thin and tapering branches rising above the wall Amaryllis was partly hidden, but she relied a great deal more for concealment upon a fact Iden had taught her, that people very seldom look up; and consequently if you are only a little higher they will not see you. This she proved that morning, for not one of all who passed glanced up from the road. The shepherd kept his eye fixed on his sheep, and the drover on his bullocks; the boys were in a hurry to get to the fair and spend their pennies; the wenches had on a bit of blue ribbon or a new bonnet, and were perpetually looking at the traps that overtook them to see if the men admired their finery. No one looked up from the road they were pursuing.

The photographer fixes the head of the sitter by a sort of stand at the back, which holds it steady in one position while the camera takes the picture. In life most people have their heads fixed in the claws of some miserable pettiness, which interests them so greatly

22

that they tramp on steadily forward, staring ahead, and there's not the slightest fear of their seeing anything outside the rut they are travelling.

Amaryllis did not care anything about the fair or the people either, knowing very well what sort they would be; but I suspect, if it had been possible to have got at the cause which brought her there, it would have been traced to the unconscious influence of sex, a perfectly innocent prompting, quite unrecognised by the person who feels it, and who would indignantly deny it if rallied on the subject, but which leads girls of her age to seize opportunities of observing the men, even if of an uninteresting order. Still they are men, those curious beings, that unknown race, and little bits of knowledge about them may, perhaps, be picked up by a diligent observer.

The men who drifted along the road towards the Fair were no "mashers, by Jove!" Some of them, though young, were clad antiquely enough in breeches and gaiters—not sportsmen's breeches and gaiters, but old-fashioned "granfer" things; the most of them were stout and sturdy, in drab and brown suits of good cloth, cut awry. Hundreds of them on foot, in traps, gigs, fourwheels, and on horseback, went under Amaryllis: but, though they were all Christians, there was not one "worth a Jewess' eye."

She scorned them all.

This member of the unknown race was too thickly made, short set, and squat; this one too fair—quite white and moist-sugar looking; this one had a straight leg.

Another went by with a great thick and long black beard—what a horrid thing, now, when kissing!—and as he walked he wiped it with his sleeve, for he had just washed down the dust with a glass of ale. His neck, too, was red and thick; hideous, yet he was a "stout knave," and a man all over, as far as body makes a man.

But women are, like Shakespeare, better judges. "Care I for the thews and sinews of a man?" They look for something more than bulk.

A good many of these fellows were more or less lame, for it is astonishing if you watch people go by and keep account of them what a number have game legs, both young and old.

A young buck on a capital horse was at the first glance more interesting—paler, rakish, a cigar in his mouth, an air of viciousness and dash combined, fairly well dressed, pale whiskers and beard; in short, he knew as much of the billiard-table as he did of sheep and corn. When nearer Amaryllis disliked him more than all the rest put together; she shrank back a little from the wall lest he should chance to look up; she would have feared to have been alone with such a

23

character, and yet she could not have said why. She would not have feared to walk side by side with the great black beard—hideous as he was—nor with any of the rest, not even with the roughest of the labourers who tramped along. This gentleman alone alarmed her.

There were two wenches, out for their Fair Day holiday, coming by at the same time; they had on their best dresses and hats, and looked fresh and nice. They turned round to watch him coming, and half waited for him; when he came up he checked his horse, and began to "cheek" them. Nothing loth, the village girls "cheeked" him, and so they passed on.

One or two very long men appeared, unusually clumsy, even in walking they did not know exactly what to do with their legs. Amaryllis had no objection to their being tall—indeed, to be tall is often a passport to a "Jewess' eye"—but they were so clumsy.

Of the scores who went by in traps and vehicles she could not see much but their clothes and their faces, and both the clothes and the faces were very much alike. Rough, good cloth, ill-fitting (the shoulders were too broad for the tailor, who wanted to force Bond Street measurements on the British farmer's back); reddish, speckled faces, and yellowish hair and whiskers; big speckled hands, and that was all. Scores of men, precisely similar, were driven down the road. If those broad speckled hands had been shown to Jacob's ewes he need not have peeled rods to make them bring forth speckled lambs.

Against the stile a long way up the road there was a group of five or six men, who were there when she first peered over the wall, and made no further progress to the Fair. They were waiting till some acquaintance came by and offered a lift; lazy dogs, they could not walk. They had already been there long enough to have walked to the Fair and back, still they preferred to fold their hands and cross their legs, and stay on. So many people being anxious to get to the town, most of those who drove had picked up friends long before they got here.

The worst walker of all was a constable, whose huge boots seemed to take possession of the width of the road, for he turned them out at right angles, working his legs sideways to do it, an extraordinary exhibition of stupidity and ugliness, for which the authorities who drilled him in that way were responsible, and not the poor fellow.

Among the lowing cattle and the baaing sheep there drifted by a variety of human animals, tramps and vagrants, not nearly of so much value as the wool and beef.

It is curious that these "characters"—as they are so kindly called—have a way of associating themselves with things that

24

promise vast enjoyment to others. The number of unhappy, shirtless wretches who thread their path in and out the coaches at the Derby is wonderful. While the champagne fizzes above on the roof, and the footman between the shafts sits on an upturned hamper and helps himself out of another to pie with truffles, the hungry, lean kine of human life wander round about sniffing and smelling, like Adam and Eve after the fall at the edge of Paradise.

There are such incredible swarms of vagrants at the Derby that you might think the race was got up entirely for their sakes. There would be thousands at Sandown, but the gate is locked with a half-crown bolt, and they cannot get a stare at the fashionables on the lawn. For all that, the true tramp, male or female, is so inveterate an attendant at races and all kinds of accessible entertainments and public events that the features of the fashionable are better known to him than to hundreds of well-to-do people unable to enter society.

So they paddled along to the fair, slip-slop, in the dust, among the cattle and sheep, hands in pockets, head hanging down, most of them followed at a short distance by a Thing.

This Thing is upright, and therefore, according to the old definition, ought to come within the genus Homo. It wears garments rudely resembling those of a woman, and there it ends. Perhaps it was a woman once; perhaps it never was, for many of them have never had a chance to enter the ranks of their own sex.

Amaryllis was too young, and, as a consequence, too full of her own strength and youth and joy in life to think for long or seriously about these curious Things drifting by like cattle and sheep. Yet her brow contracted, and she drew herself together as they passed—a sort of shiver, to think that there should be such degradation in the world. Twice when they came along her side of the road she dropped pennies in front of them, which they picked up in a listless way, just glancing over the ear in the direction the money fell, and went on without so much as recognizing where it came from.

If sheep were treated as unfortunate human beings are, they would take a bitter revenge; though they are the mildest of creatures, they would soon turn round in a venomous manner. If they did not receive sufficient to eat and drink, and were not well sheltered, they would take a bitter revenge: they would die. Loss of £ s. d.!

But human beings have not even got the courage or energy to do that; they put up with anything, and drag on—miserables that they are.

I said they were not equal in value to the sheep—why, they're

25

not worth anything when they're dead. You cannot even sell the skins of the Things!

Slip-slop in the dust they drive along to the fair, where there will be an immense amount of eating and a far larger amount of drinking all round them, in every house they pass, and up to midnight. They will see valuable animals, and men with well-lined pockets. What on earth can a tramp find to please him among all this? It is not for him; yet he goes to see it.

CHAPTER VII

THE crowd began to pass more thickly, when Amaryllis saw a man coming up the road in the opposite direction to that in which the multitude was moving. They were going to the fair; he had his back to it, and a party in a trap rallied him smartly for his folly.

"What! bean't you a-going to fair? Why, Measter Duck, what's up? Looking for a thunderstorm?"—which young ducks are supposed to enjoy. "Ha! ha! ha!"

Measter Duck, with a broad grin on his face, nevertheless plodded up the hill, and passed beneath Amaryllis.

She knew him very well, for he lived in the hamlet, but she would not have taken any notice of him had he not been so elaborately dressed. His high silk hat shone glossy; his black broadcloth coat was new and carefully brushed; he was in black all over, in contrast with the mass of people who had gone by that morning. A blue necktie, bright and clean, spotless linen, gloves rolled up in a ball in one hand, whiskers brushed, boots shining, teeth clean, Johnny was off to the fair!

The coat fitted him to a nicety; it had, in fact, no chance to do otherwise, for his great back and shoulders stretched it tight, and would have done so had it been made like a sack. Of all the big men who had gone by that day Jack Duck was the biggest; his back was immense, and straight, too, for he walked upright for a farmer, nor was his bulk altogether without effect, for he was not over-burdened with abdomen, so that it showed to the best advantage. He was a little over the average height, but not tall; he had grown laterally.

He could lift two sacks of wheat from the ground. You just try to lift one.

His sleeves were too long, so that only the great knuckles of his speckled hands were visible. Red whiskers, red hair, blue eyes, speckled face, straight lips, thick, like the edge of an earthenware pitcher, and of much the same coarse red hue, always a ready grin, a round, hard head, which you might have hit safely with a mallet; and there is the picture.

For some reason, very big men do not look well in glossy black coats and silk hats; they seem to want wideawakes, bowlers, caps, anything rather than a Paris hat, and some loose-cut jacket of a free-and-easy colour, suitable for the field, or cricket, or boating. They do not belong to the town and narrow doorways; Nature grew them for hills and fields.

Compared with the Continental folk, most Englishmen are big, and therefore, as their "best" suits do not fit in with their character as written in limbs and shoulders, the Continent thinks us clumsy. The truth is, it is the Continent that is little.

"Isn't he ugly?" thought Amaryllis, looking down on poor John Duck. "Isn't he ugly?" Now the top of the wall was crusted with moss, which has a way of growing into bricks and mortar, and attaching particles of brick to its roots. As she watched the people she unconsciously trifled with a little piece of moss—her hand happened at the moment to project over the wall, and as John Duck went under she dropped the bit of moss straight on his glossy hat. Tap! the fragment of brick adhering to the moss struck the hollow hat smartly like a drum.

She drew back quickly, laughing and blushing, and angry with herself all at the same time, for she had done it without a thought.

Jack pulled off his hat, saw nothing, and put it on again, suspecting that some one in a passing gig had "chucked" something at him.

In a minute Amaryllis peeped over the wall, and, seeing his broad back a long way up the road, resumed her stand.

"How ever could I do such a stupid thing?" she thought. "But isn't he ugly? Aren't they all ugly? All of them—horridly ugly."

The entire unknown race of Man was hideous. So coarse in feature—their noses were thick, half an inch thick, or enormously long and knobbed at the end like a walking-stick, or curved like a reaping-hook, or slewed to one side, or flat as if they had been smashed, or short and stumpy and incomplete, or spotted with red blotches, or turned up in the vulgarest manner—nobody had a good nose.

Their eyes were goggles, round and staring—like liquid

marbles—they had no eyelashes, and their eyebrows were either white and invisible, or shaggy, as if thistles grew along their foreheads.

Their cheeks were speckled and freckled and red and brick-dust and leather-coloured, and enclosed with scrubby whiskers, like a garden hedge.

Upon the whole, those who shaved and were smooth looked worse than those who did not, for they thus exposed the angularities of their chins and jaws.

They wore such horrid hats on the top of these roughly-sketched faces—sketched, as it were, with a bit of burnt stick. Some of them had their hats on the backs of their heads, and some wore them aslant, and some jammed over their brows.

They went along smoking and puffing, and talking and guffawing in the vulgarest way, en route to swill and smoke and puff and guffaw somewhere else.

Whoever could tell what they were talking about? these creatures.

They had no form or grace like a woman—no lovely sloped shoulders, no beautiful bosom, no sweeping curve of robe down to the feet. No softness of cheek, or silky hair, or complexion, or taper fingers, or arched eyebrows; no sort of style whatever. They were mere wooden figures; and, in short, sublimely ugly.

There was a good deal of truth in Amaryllis' reflections; it was a pity a woman was not taken into confidence when the men were made.

Suppose the women were like the men, and we had to make love to such a set of bristly, grisly wretches!—pah! shouldn't we think them ugly! The patience of the women, putting up with us so long!

As for the muscles on which we pride ourselves so much, in a woman's eyes (though she prefers a strong man) they simply increase our extraordinary ugliness.

But if we look pale, and slim, and so forth, then they despise us, and there is no doubt that altogether the men were made wrong.

"And Jack's the very ugliest of the lot," thought Amaryllis. "He just is ugly."

Pounding up the slope, big John Duck came by-and-by to the gateway, and entering without ceremony, as is the custom in the country, found Mr. Iden near the back door talking to a farmer who had seated himself on a stool.

He was a middle-aged man, stout and florid, rough as a chunk of wood, but dressed in his best brown for the fair. Tears were rolling down his vast round cheeks as he expatiated on his grievances to Mr. Iden:—

"Now, just you see how I be helped up with this here 'ooman," he concluded as Duck arrived. Mr. Iden, not a little glad of an opportunity to escape a repetition of the narrative, to which he had patiently listened, took Jack by the arm, and led him indoors. As they went the man on the stool extended his arm towards them hopelessly:—"Just you see how I be helped up with this here 'ooman!"

A good many have been "helped up" with a woman before now.

Mrs. Iden met Jack with a gracious smile—she always did—yet there could not have been imagined a man less likely to have pleased her.

A quick, nervous temperament, an eye sharp to detect failings or foolishness, an admirer of briskness and vivacity, why did she welcome John Duck, that incarnation of stolidity and slowness, that enormous mountain of a man? Because extremes meet? No, since she was always complaining of Iden's dull, motionless life; so it was not the contrast to her own disposition that charmed her.

John Duck was Another Man—not Mr. Iden.

The best of matrons like to see Another Man enter their houses; there's no viciousness in it, it is simply nature, which requires variety. The best of husbands likes to have another woman—or two, or three—on a visit; there's nothing wrong, it is innocent enough, and but gives a spice to the monotony of existence.

Besides, John Duck, that mountain of slowness and stolidity, was not perhaps a fool, notwithstanding his outward clumsiness. A little attention is appreciated even by a matron of middle age.

"Will you get us some ale?" said Iden; and Mrs. Iden brought a full jug with her own hands—a rare thing, for she hated the Goliath barrel as Iden enjoyed it.

"Going to the fair, Mr. Duck?"

"Yes, m'm," said John, deep in his chest and gruff, about as a horse might be expected to speak if he had a voice. "You going, m'm? I just come up to ask if you'd ride in my dog-trap?"

John had a first-rate turn-out.

Mrs. Iden, beaming with smiles, replied that she was not going to the fair.

"Should be glad to take you, you know," said John, dipping into the ale. "Shall you be going presently?"—to Mr. Iden. "Perhaps you'd have a seat?"

"Hum!" said Iden, fiddling with his chin, a trick he had when

29

undecided. "I don't zactly know; fine day, you see; want to see that hedge grubbed; want to fill up the gaps; want to go over to the wood meads; thought about——"

"There, take and go!" said Mrs. Iden. "Sit there thinking—take and go."

"I can't say zactly, John; don't seem to have anything to go vor."

"What do other people go for?" said Mrs. Iden, contemptuously. "Why can't you do like other people? Get on your clean shirt, and go. Jack can wait—he can talk to Amaryllis while you dress."

"Perhaps Miss would like to go," suggested John, very quietly, and as if it was no consequence to him; the very thing he had called for, to see if he could get Amaryllis to drive in with him. He knew that Mrs. Iden never went anywhere, and that Mr. Iden could not make up his mind in a minute—he would require three or four days at least—so that it was quite safe to ask them first.

"Of course she would," said Mrs. Iden. "She is going—to dine with her grandfather; it will save her a long walk. You had better go and ask her; she's down at Plum Corner, watching the people."

"So I wull," said Jack, looking out of the great bow window at the mention of Plum Corner—he could just see the flutter of Amaryllis' dress in the distance between the trees. That part of the garden was called Plum Corner because of a famous plum tree—the one that had not been pruned and was sprawling about the wall.

Mr. Iden had planted that plum tree specially for Mrs. Iden, because she was so fond of a ripe luscious plum. But of late years he had not pruned it.

"Vine ale!" said John, finishing his mug. "Extra vine ale!"

"It be, bean't it?" said Mr. Iden.

It really was humming stuff, but John well knew how proud Iden was of it, and how much he liked to hear it praised.

The inhabitants of the City of London conceitedly imagine that no one can be sharp-witted outside the sound of Bow Bells—country people are stupid. My opinion is that clumsy Jack Duck, who took about half an hour to write his name, was equal to most of them.

CHAPTER VIII

THE ale being ended, Iden walked with him through the orchard.

"Famous wall that," said John, presently, nodding towards the great red brick wall which adorned that side of the place. "Knowed how to build walls in those days."

"No such wall as that anywhere about here," said Iden, as proud of his wall as his ale. "No such bricks to be got. Folk don't know how to put up a wall now—you read in the papers how the houses valls down in Lunnon."

"Sort of cracks and comes in like—jest squashes up," said John.

"Now, that's a real bit of brickwork," said Iden. "That'll last— ah, last——"

"No end to it," said John, who had admired the wall forty times before, thinking to himself as he saw Amaryllis leaning over the corner, "Blessed if I don't think as 'twas she as dropped summat on my hat." This strengthened his hopes; he had a tolerably clear idea that Mr. and Mrs. Iden were not averse to his suit; but he was doubtful about Amaryllis herself.

Amaryllis had not the slightest idea Duck had so much as looked at her—he called often, but seemed absorbed in the ale and gossip. Fancy her scorn if she had guessed!

John Duck was considered one of the most eligible young men thereabouts, for though by no means born in the purple of farming, it was believed he was certain to be very "warm" indeed when his father died. Old Duck, the son of a common labourer, occupied two or three of the finest farms in the neighbourhood. He made his money in a waggon—a curious place, you will say; why so? Have you ever seen the dingy, dark china-closets they call offices in the City? Have you ever ascended the dirty, unscrubbed, disgraceful staircase that leads to a famous barrister's "chambers"? These are far less desirable, surely, than a seat in a waggon in a beautiful meadow or cornfield. Old Duck, being too ponderous to walk, was driven about in a waggon, sitting at the rear with his huge, short legs dangling down; and, the waggon being halted in a commanding position, he overlooked his men at work.

One day he was put in a cart instead, and the carter walking home beside the horse, and noting what a pull it was for him up the hills, and drawling along half asleep, quite forgot his master, and dreamed he had a load of stones. By-and-by, he pulled out the bar, and shot Old Duck out. "A shot me out," grumbled the old man, "as if I'd a been a load of flints."

Riding about in this rude chariot the old fellow had amassed considerable wealth—his reputation for money was very great indeed—and his son John would, of course, come in for it.

John felt sure of Mr. and Mrs. Iden, but about Amaryllis he did not know. The idea that she had dropped "summat" on his hat raised his spirits immensely.

Now Amaryllis was not yet beautiful—she was too young; I do not think any girl is really beautiful so young—she was highly individualized, and had a distinct character, as it were, in her face and figure. You saw at a glance that there was something about her very different from other girls, something very marked, but it was not beauty yet.

Whether John thought her handsome, or saw that she would be, or what, I do not know; or whether he looked "forrard," as he would have said.

"Heigh for a lass with a tocher!"

John had never read Burns, and would not have known that tocher meant dowry; nor had he seen the advice of Tennyson—

"Doesn't thee marry for money,
But go where money lies."

but his native intelligence needed no assistance from the poets, coronetted or otherwise.

It was patent to everyone that her father, Iden, was as poor as the raggedest coat in Christendom could make him; but it was equally well known and a matter of public faith, that her grandfather, the great miller and baker, Lord Lardy-Cake, as the boys called him derisively, had literally bushels upon bushels of money. He was a famous stickler for ancient usages, and it was understood that there were twenty thousand spade guineas in an iron box under his bed. Any cottager in the whole country side could have told you so, and would have smiled at your ignorance; the thing was as well known as that St. Paul's is in the City.

Besides which there was another consideration, old Granfer Iden was a great favourite at Court—Court meaning the mansion of the Hon. Raleigh Pamment, the largest landowner that side of the county. Granfer Iden entered the Deer Park (which was private) with a special key whenever he pleased, he strolled about the gardens, looked in at the conservatory, chatted familiarly with the royal family of Pamment when they were at home, and when they were away took any friend he chose through the galleries and saloons.

"Must be summat at the bottom on't," said John Duck to himself many a time and oft. "They stuck-up proud folk wouldn't have he there if there wasn't summat at the bottom on't." A favourite at Court could dispense, no doubt, many valuable privileges.

Amaryllis heard their talk as they came nearer, and turned round and faced them. She wore a black dress, but no hat; instead she had carelessly thrown a scarlet shawl over her head, mantilla fashion, and held it with one hand. Her dark ringlets fringed her forehead, blown free and wild; the fresh air had brought a bright colour into her cheeks. As is often the case with girls whose figure is just beginning to show itself, her dress seemed somewhat shortened in front—lifted up from her ankles, which gave the effect of buoyancy to her form, she seemed about to walk though standing still. There was a defiant light in her deep brown eyes, that sort of "I don't care" disposition which our grandmothers used to say would take us to the gallows. Defiance, wilfulness, rebellion, was expressed in the very way she stood on the bank, a little higher than they were, and able to look over their heads.

"Marning," said John, rocking his head to one side as a salute.

"Marning," repeated Amaryllis, mocking his broad pronunciation.

As John could not get any further Iden helped him.

"Jack's going to the fair," he said, "and thought you would like to ride with him. Run in and dress."

"I shan't ride," said Amaryllis, "I shall walk."

"Longish way," said John. "Mor'n two mile."

"I shall walk," said Amaryllis, decidedly.

"Lot of cattle about," said John.

"Better ride," said Iden.

"No," said Amaryllis, and turned her back on them to look over the wall again.

She was a despot already. There was nothing left for them but to walk away.

"However," said Iden, always trying to round things off and make square edges smooth, "very likely you'll overtake her and pick her up."

"Her wull go across the fields," said John. "Shan't see her."

As he walked down the road home for his dog-trap he looked

up at the corner of the wall, but she was not looking over then. Mrs. Iden had fetched her in, as it was time to dress.

"I don't want to go," said Amaryllis, "I hate fairs—they are so silly."

"But you must go," said Mrs. Iden. "Your grandfather sent a message last night; you know it's his dinner-day."

"He's such a horrid old fellow," said Amaryllis, "I can't bear him."

"How dare you speak of your grandfather like that? you are getting very rude and disrespectful."

There was no depending on Mrs. Iden. At one time she would go on and abuse Granfer Iden for an hour at a time, calling him every name she could think of, and accusing him of every folly under the sun. At another time she would solemnly inform Amaryllis that they had not a farthing of money, and how necessary it was that they should be attentive and civil to him.

Amaryllis very slowly put her hat on and the first jacket to hand.

"What! aren't you going to change your dress?"

"No, that I'm not."

"Change it directly."

"What, to go in and see that musty old——"

"Change it directly; I will be obeyed."

Amaryllis composedly did as she was bid.

One day Mrs. Iden humoured her every whim and let her do just as she pleased; the next she insisted on minute obedience.

"Make haste, you'll be late; now, then, put your things on—come."

So Amaryllis, much against her will, was bustled out of the house and started off. As John had foreseen, she soon quitted the road to follow the path across the fields, which was shorter.

An hour or so later Iden came in from work as usual, a few minutes before dinner, and having drawn his quart of ale, sat down to sip it in the bow window till the dishes were brought.

"You're not gone, then?" said Mrs. Iden, irritatingly.

"Gone—wur?" said Iden, rather gruffly for him.

"To fair, of course—like other people."

"Hum," growled Iden.

"You know your father expects all the family to come in to dinner on fair day; I can't think how you can neglect him, when you know we haven't got a shilling—why don't you go in and speak to him?"

"You can go if you like."

"I go!" cried Mrs. Iden. "I go!" in shrill accents of contempt. "I

34

don't care a button for all the lardy-cake lot! Let him keep his money. I'm as good as he is any day. My family go about, and do some business——"

"Your family," muttered Iden. "The Flammas!"

"Yes, my family—as good as yours, I should think! What's your family then, that you should be so grand? You're descended from a lardy-cake!"

"You be descended from a quart pot," said Iden.

This was an allusion to Mrs. Iden's grandfather, who had kept a small wayside public. There was no disgrace in it, for he was a very respectable man, and laid the foundation of his family's fortune, but it drove Mrs. Iden into frenzy.

"You talk about a quart pot—you," she shrieked. "Why, your family have drunk up thousands of pounds—you know they have. Where's the Manor? they swilled it away. Where's Upper Court? they got it down their throats. They built a house to drink in and nothing else. You know they did. You told me yourself. The most disgraceful set of drunkards that ever lived!"

"Your family don't drink, then, I suppose?" said Iden.

"Your lot's been drinking two hundred years—why, you're always talking about it."

"Your family be as nervous as cats—see their hands shake in the morning."

"They go to business in the City and do something; they don't mess about planting rubbishing potatoes." Mrs. Iden was London born.

"A pretty mess they've made of their business, as shaky as their hands. Fidgetty, miserable, nervous set they be."

"They're not stocks and stones like yours, anyhow, as stolid, and slow, and stupid; why, you do nothing but sleep, sleep, sleep, and talk, talk, talk. You've been talking with the lazy lot over at the stile, and you've been talking with that old fool at the back door, and talking with Jack Duck—and that's your second mug! You're descended from a nasty, greasy lardy-cake! There!"

Iden snatched a piece of bread from the table and thrust it in one pocket, flung open the oven-door, and put a baked apple in the other pocket, and so marched out to eat what he could in quiet under a tree in the fields.

In the oratory of abuse there is no resource so successful as raking up the weaknesses of the opponent's family, especially when the parties are married, for having gossiped with each other for so long in the most confidential manner, they know every foible. How Robert drank, and Tom bet, and Sam swore, and Bill knocked his wife about, and Joseph did as Potiphar's spouse asked him, and why

35

your uncle had to take refuge in Spain; and so on to an indefinite extent, like the multiplication table.

CHAPTER IX

THIS discordance between her father and mother hurt Amaryllis' affectionate heart exceedingly. It seemed to be always breaking out all the year round.

Of a summer's eve, when the day's work among the hot hay was done, Iden would often go out and sit under the russet apple till the dew had filled the grass like a green sea. When the tide of the dew had risen he would take off his heavy boots and stockings, and so walk about in the cool shadows of eve, paddling in the wet grass. He liked the refreshing coolness and the touch of the sward. It was not for washing, because he was scrupulously clean under the ragged old coat; it was because he liked the grass. There was nothing very terrible in it; men, and women, too, take off their shoes and stockings, and wade about on the sands at the sea, and no one thinks that it is anything but natural, reasonable, and pleasant. But, then, you see, everybody does it at the seaside, and Iden alone waded in the dew, and that was his crime—that he alone did it.

The storm and rage of Mrs. Iden whenever she knew he was paddling in the grass was awful. She would come shuffling out—she had a way of rubbing her shoes along the ground when irritated with her hands under her apron, which she twisted about—and pelt him with scorn.

"There, put your boots on—do, and hide your nasty feet!" (Iden had a particularly white skin, and feet as white as a lady's.) "Disgusting! Nobody ever does it but you, and you ought to be ashamed of yourself! Anything more disgusting I never heard of. Nobody else but you would ever think of such a thing; makes me feel queer to see you."

Shuffling about, and muttering to herself, "Nobody else"—that was the sin and guilt of it—by-and-by Mrs. Iden would circle round to where he had left his boots, and, suddenly seizing them, would fling them in the ditch.

And I verily believe, in the depth of her indignation, if she had

36

not been afraid to touch firearms, she would have brought out the gun, and had a shot at him.

After a time Iden left his old post at the russet apple, and went up the meadow to the horse-chestnut trees that he himself had planted, and there, in peace and quietness and soft cool shadow, waded about in the dew, without any one to grumble at him.

How crookedly things are managed in this world!

It is the modern fashion to laugh at the East, and despise the Turks and all their ways, making Grand Viziers of barbers, and setting waiters in high places, with the utmost contempt for anything reasonable—all so incongruous and chance-ruled. In truth, all things in our very midst go on in the Turkish manner; crooked men are set in straight places, and straight people in crooked places, just the same as if we had all been dropped promiscuously out of a bag and shook down together on the earth to work out our lives, quite irrespective of our abilities and natures. Such an utter jumble!

Here was Iden, with his great brain and wonderful power of observation, who ought to have been a famous traveller in unexplored Africa or Thibet, bringing home rarities and wonders; or, with his singular capacity for construction, a leading engineer, boring Mont Cenis Tunnels and making Panama Canals; or, with his Baconian intellect, forming a new school of philosophy—here was Iden, tending cows, and sitting, as the old story goes, undecidedly on a stile—sitting astride—eternally sitting, and unable to make up his mind to get off on one side or the other.

Here was Mrs. Iden, who had had a beautiful shape and expressive eyes, full in her youth of life and fire, who ought to have led the gayest life in London and Paris alternately, riding in a carriage, and flinging money about in the most extravagant, joyous, and good-natured manner—here was Mrs. Iden making butter in a dull farmhouse, and wearing shoes out at the toes.

So our lives go on, rumble-jumble, like a carrier's cart over ruts and stones, thumping anyhow instead of running smoothly on new-mown sward like a cricket-ball.

It all happens in the Turkish manner.

Another time there would come a letter from one of the Flammas in London. Could they spare a little bag of lavender?—they grew such lovely sweet lavender at Coombe Oaks. Then you might see Mr. and Mrs. Iden cooing and billing, soft as turtle-doves, and fraternising in the garden over the lavender hedge. Here was another side, you see, to the story.

Mrs. Iden was very fond of lavender, the scent, and the plant in every form. She kept little bags of it in all her drawers, and everything at Coombe Oaks upstairs in the bedrooms had a faint, delicious lavender perfume. There is nothing else that smells so sweet and clean and dry. You cannot imagine a damp sheet smelling of lavender.

Iden himself liked lavender, and used to rub it between his finger and thumb in the garden, as he did, too, with the black-currant leaves and walnut-leaves, if he fancied anything he had touched might have left an unpleasant odour adhering to his skin. He said it cleaned his hands as much as washing them.

Iden liked Mrs. Iden to like lavender because his mother had been so fond of it, and all the sixteen carved oak-presses which had been so familiar to him in boyhood were full of a thick atmosphere of the plant.

Long since, while yet the honeymoon bouquet remained in the wine of life, Iden had set a hedge of lavender to please his wife. It was so carefully chosen, and set, and watched, that it grew to be the finest lavender in all the country. People used to come for it from round about, quite certain of a favourable reception, for there was nothing so sure to bring peace at Coombe Oaks as a mention of lavender.

But the letter from the Flammas was the great event—from London, all that way, asking for some Coombe Oaks lavender! Then there was billing and cooing, and fraternising, and sunshine in the garden over the hedge of lavender. If only it could have lasted! Somehow, as people grow older there seems so much grating of the wheels.

In time, long time, people's original feelings get strangely confused and overlaid. The churchwardens of the eighteenth century plastered the fresco paintings of the fourteenth in their churches—covered them over with yellowish mortar. The mould grows up, and hides the capital of the fallen column; the acanthus is hidden in earth. At the foot of the oak, where it is oldest, the bark becomes dense and thick, impenetrable, and without sensitiveness; you may cut off an inch thick without reaching the sap. A sort of scale or caking in long, long time grows over original feelings.

There was no one in the world so affectionate and loving as Mrs. Iden—no one who loved a father so dearly; just as Amaryllis loved her father.

But after they had lived at Coombe Oaks thirty years or so, and the thick dull bark had grown, after the scales or caking had come upon the heart, after the capital of the column had fallen, after the painting had been blurred, it came about that old Flamma, Mrs. Iden's father, died in London.

After thirty years of absolute quiet at Coombe Oaks, husband and wife went up to London to the funeral, which took place at one of those fearful London cemeteries that strike a chill at one's very soul. Of all the horrible things in the world there is nothing so calmly ghastly as a London cemetery.

In the evening, after the funeral, Mr. and Mrs. Iden went to the theatre.

"How frivolous! How unfeeling!" No, nothing of the sort; how truly sad and human, for to be human is to be sad. That men and women should be so warped and twisted by the pressure of the years out of semblance to themselves; that circumstances should so wall in their lives with insurmountable cliffs of granite facts, compelling them to tread the sunless gorge; that the coldness of death alone could open the door to pleasure.

They sat at the theatre with grey hearts. With the music and the song, the dancing, the colours and gay dresses, it was sadder there than in the silent rooms at the house where the dead had been. Old Flamma alone had been dead there; they were dead here. Dead in life—at the theatre.

They had used to go joyously to the theatre thirty years before, when Iden came courting to town; from the edge of the grave they came back to look on their own buried lives.

If you will only think, you will see it was a most dreadful and miserable incident, that visit to the theatre after the funeral.

CHAPTER X

WHEN Mrs. Iden threw his lardy-cake descent in Iden's face she alluded to Grandfather Iden's being a baker and miller, and noted for the manufacture of these articles. A lardy, or larded, cake is a thing, I suppose, unknown to most of this generation; they were the principal confectionery familiar to country folk when Grandfather Iden was at the top of his business activity, seventy years since, in the Waterloo era.

A lardy-cake is an oblong, flat cake, crossed with lines, and rounded at the corners, made of dough, lard, sugar, and spice. Our ancestors liked something to gnaw at, and did not go in for lightness in their pastry; they liked something to stick to their teeth, and after that to their ribs. The lardy-cake eminently fulfilled these

39

conditions; they put a trifle of sugar and spice in it, to set it going as it were, and the rest depended on the strength of the digestion. But if a ploughboy could get a new, warm lardy-cake, fresh from the oven, he thought himself blessed.

Grandfather Iden had long since ceased any serious business, but he still made a few of these renowned cakes for his amusement, and sold a good few at times to the carters' lads who came in to market.

Amaryllis knew the path perfectly, but if she had not, the tom-tomming of drums and blowing of brass, audible two miles away, would have guided her safely to the fair. The noise became prodigious as she approached—the ceaseless tomtom, the beating of drums and gongs outside the show vans, the shouting of the showmen, the roar of a great crowd, the booing of cattle, the baaing of sheep, the neighing of horses—altogether the "rucket" was tremendous.

She looked back from the hill close to the town and saw the people hurrying in from every quarter—there was a string of them following the path she had come, and others getting over distant stiles. A shower had fallen in the night, but the ceaseless wheels had ground up the dust again, and the lines of the various roads were distinctly marked by the clouds hanging above them. For one on business, fifty hastened on to join the uproar.

Suppose the Venus de Medici had been fetched from Florence and had been set up in the town of Woolhorton, or the Laocoon from Rome, or the Milo from Paris, do you think all these people would have scurried in such haste to admire these beautiful works? Nothing of the sort; if you want a crowd you must make a row. It is really wonderful how people do thoroughly and unaffectedly enjoy a fearful disturbance; if the cannon could be shot off quietly, and guns made no noise, battles would not be half so popular to read about. The silent arrow is uninteresting, and if you describe a mediæval scramble you must put in plenty of splintering lances, resounding armour, shrieks and groans, and so render it lively.

"This is the patent age of new inventions," and some one might make a profit by starting a fête announcing that a drum or a gong would be provided for every individual, to be beaten in a grand universal chorus.

Amaryllis had no little difficulty in getting through the crowd till she found her way behind the booths and slipped along the narrow passage between them and the houses. There was an arched entrance, archæologically interesting, by which she paused a moment, half inclined to go up and inquire for her boots. The shoemaker who lived there had had them since Christmas, and all that wanted doing was a patch on one toe; they were always just going to be done, but never finished. She read the inscription over his door, "Tiras Wise, Shoemaker; Established 1697." A different sort of shoemaker to your lively Northampton awls; a man who has been in business two hundred years cannot be hurried. She sighed, and passed on.

The step to Grandfather Iden's door consisted of one wide stone of semi-circular shape, in which the feet of three generations of customers had worn a deep grove. The venerable old gentleman, for he was over ninety, was leaning on the hatch (or lower half of the door), in the act of handing some of his cakes to two village girls who had called for them. These innocent, hamlet girls, supposed to be so rurally simple, had just been telling him how they never forgot his nice cakes, but always came every fair day to buy some. For this they got sixpence each, it being well known that the old gentleman was so delighted with anybody who bought his cakes he generally gave them back their money, and a few coppers besides.

He took Amaryllis by the arm as she stood on the step and pulled her into the shop, asked her if her father were coming, then walked her down by the oven-door, and made her stand up by a silver-mounted peel, to see how tall she was. The peel is the long wooden rod, broad at one end, with which loaves are placed in the baker's oven. Father Iden being proud of his trade, in his old age had his favourite peel ornamented with silver.

"Too fast—too fast," he said, shaking his head, and coughing; "you grow too fast; there's the notch I cut last year, and now you're two inches taller." He lowered the peel, and showed her where his thumb was—quite two inches higher than the last year's mark.

"I want to be tall," said Amaryllis.

"I daresay—I daresay," said the old man, in the hasty manner of feeble age, as he cut another notch to record her height. The handle of the peel was notched all round, where he had measured his grandchildren; there were so many marks it was not easy to see how he distinguished them.

"Is your father coming?" he asked, when he had finished with the knife.

"I don't know." This was Jesuitically true—she did not know—she could not be certain; but in her heart she was sure he would not come. But she did not want to hear any hard words said about him.

"Has he sent anything? Have you brought anything for me? No. No. Hum!—ha!"—fit of coughing—"Well, well—come in; dinner's late, there's time to hear you read—you're fond of books, you read a great deal at home,"—and so talking, half to himself and half to her, he led the way into the parlour by the shop.

41

Bowed by more than ninety years, his back curved over forwards, and his limbs curved in the opposite direction, so that the outline of his form resembled a flattened capital S. For his chin hung over his chest, and his knees never straightened themselves, but were always more or less bent as he stood or walked. It was much the attitude of a strong man heavily laden and unable to stand upright—such an attitude as big Jack Duck in his great strength might take when carrying two sacks of wheat at once. There was as heavy a load on Grandfather Iden's back, but Time is invisible.

He wore a grey suit, as a true miller and baker should, and had worn the same cut and colour for years and years. In the shop, too, he always had a grey hat on, perhaps its original hue was white, but it got to appear grey upon him; a large grey chimney-pot, many sizes too big for his head apparently, for it looked as if for ever about to descend and put out his face like an extinguisher. Though his boots were so carefully polished, they quickly took a grey tint from the flour dust as he pottered about the bins in the morning. The ends of his trousers, too long for his antique shanks, folded and creased over his boots, and almost hid his grey cloth under-gaiters.

A great knobbed old nose—but stay, I will not go further, it is not right to paint too faithfully the features of the very aged, which are repellent in spite of themselves; I mean, they cannot help their faces, their sentiments and actions are another matter; therefore I will leave Father Iden's face as a dim blot on the mirror; you look in it and it reflects everywhere, except one spot.

Amaryllis followed him jauntily,—little did she care, reckless girl, for the twenty thousand guineas in the iron box under his bed.

The cottage folk, who always know so much, had endless tales of Iden's wealth; how years ago bushels upon bushels of pennies, done up in five-shilling packets, had been literally carted like potatoes away from the bakehouse to go to London; how ponies were laden with sacks of silver groats, all paid over that furrowed counter for the golden flour, dust more golden than the sands of ancient Pactolus.

Reckless Amaryllis cared not a pin for all the spade guineas in the iron box.

The old man sat down by the fire without removing his hat, motioning to her to shut the door, which she was loth to do, for the little room was smothered with smoke. Troubled with asthma, he coughed incessantly, and mopped his mouth with a vast silk handkerchief, but his dull blood craved for warmth, and he got his knees close to the grate, and piled up the coal till it smoked and smoked, and filled the close apartment with a suffocating haze of carbon. To be asked into Father Iden's sanctuary was an honour, but, like other honours, it had to be paid for.

Amaryllis gasped as she sat down, and tried to breathe as short as possible, to avoid inhaling more than she could bear.

"Books," said her grandfather, pointing to the bookcases, which occupied three sides of the room. "Books—you like books; look at them—go and see."

To humour him, Amaryllis rose, and appeared to look carefully along the shelves which she had scanned so many times before. They contained very good books indeed, such books as were not to be found elsewhere throughout the whole town of Woolhorton, and perhaps hardly in the county, old and rare volumes of price, such as Sotheby, Wilkinson, and Co. delight to offer to collectors, such as Bernard Quaritch, that giant of the modern auction room, would have written magnificent cheques for.

Did you ever see the Giant Quaritch in the auction-room bidding for books? It is one of the sights of London, let me tell you, to any one who thinks or is alive to the present day. Most sights are reputations merely—the pale reflection of things that were real once. This sight is something of the living time, the day in which we live. Get an Athenæum in the season, examine the advertisements of book auctions, and attend the next great sale of some famous library.

You have a recollection of the giant who sat by the highway and devoured the pilgrims who passed? This giant sits in the middle of the ring and devours the books set loose upon their travels after the repose of centuries.

What prices to give! No one can withstand him. From Paris they send agents with a million francs at their back; from Berlin and Vienna come the eager snappers-up of much considered trifles, but in vain. They only get what the Giant chooses to leave them.

Books that nobody ever heard of fetch £50, £60, £100, £200; wretched little books never opened since they were printed; dull duodecimos on the course of the river Wein; nondescript indescribable twaddling local books in Italian, Spanish, queer French, written and printed in some unknown foreign village; read them—you might as well try to amuse yourself with a Chinese pamphlet! What earthly value they are of cannot be discovered. They were composed by authors whose names are gone like the sand washed by the Nile into the sea before Herodotus. They contain no beautiful poetry, no elevated thought, no scientific discovery; they are simply so much paper, printing, and binding, so many years old, and it is for that age, printing, and binding that the money is paid.

43

I have read a good many books in my time—I would not give sixpence for the whole lot.

They are not like a block-book—first efforts at printing; nor like the first editions of great authors; there is not the slightest intrinsic value in them whatever.

Yet some of them fetch prices which not long ago were thought tremendous even for the Shakespeare folio.

Hundreds and hundreds of pounds are paid for them. Living and writing authors of the present day are paid in old songs by comparison.

Still, this enormous value set on old books is one of the remarkable signs of the day. If any one wishes to know what To-Day is, these book-auctions are of the things he should go to see.

Such books as these lined Grandfather Iden's shelves; among them there were a few that I call real old books, an early translation or two, an early Shakespeare, and once there had been a very valuable Boccaccio, but this had gone into Lord Pamment's library, "Presented by James Bartholomew Iden, Esq."

The old man often went to look at and admire his Boccaccio in my Lord's library.

CHAPTER XI

THERE was one peculiarity in all the books on Grandfather Iden's shelves, they were all very finely bound in the best style of hand-art, and they all bore somewhere or other a little design of an ancient Roman lamp.

Hand-art is a term I have invented for the workmanship of good taste—it is not the sculptor's art, nor the painter's—not the art of the mind, but the art of the hand. Some furniture and cabinet work, for instance, some pottery, book-binding like this, are the products of hand-art.

"Do you see the Lamp?" asked the old man, when Amaryllis had stared sufficiently at the backs of the books.

"Yes, I can see the Lamp."

"House of Flamma," said old Iden.

"House of Flamma," repeated Amaryllis, hastily, eager to

44

show that she understood all about it. She feared lest he should enter into the history of the House of Flamma and of his connection with it; she had heard it all over and over again; her mother was a Flamma; she had herself some of the restless Flamma blood in her. When anything annoyed her or made her indignant her foot used to tap the floor, and her neck flush rosy, and her face grow dusky like the night. Then, striving to control herself, she would say to herself, "I will not be a Flamma."

Except her dear mother and one other, Amaryllis detested and despised the whole tribe of the Flammas, the nervous, excitable, passionate, fidgetty, tipsy, idle, good-for-nothing lot; she hated them all, the very name and mention of them; she sided with her father as an Iden against her mother's family, the Flammas. True they were almost all flecked with talent like white foam on a black horse, a spot or two of genius, and the rest black guilt or folly. She hated them; she would not be a Flamma.

How should she at sixteen understand the wear and tear of life, the pressure of circumstances, the heavy weight of difficulties— there was something to be said even for the miserable fidgetty Flammas, but naturally sixteen judged by appearances. Shut up in narrow grooves and working day after day, year after year, in a contracted way, by degrees their constitutional nervousness became the chief characteristic of their existence. It was Intellect overcome—over-burdened—with two generations of petty cares; Genius dulled and damped till it went to the quart pot.

Sixteen could scarcely understand this. Amaryllis detested the very name; she would not be a Flamma.

But she was a Flamma for all that; a Flamma in fire of spirit, in strength of indignation, in natural capacity; she drew, for instance, with the greatest ease in pencil or pen-and-ink, drew to the life; she could write a letter in sketches.

Her indignation sometimes at the wrongfulness of certain things seemed to fill her with a consuming fire. Her partizanship for her father made her sometimes inwardly rage for the lightning, that she might utterly erase the opposer. Her contempt of sycophancy, and bold independence led her constantly into trouble.

Flamma means a flame.

Yet she was gentleness itself too; see her at the bookshelves patiently endeavouring to please the tiresome old man.

"Open that drawer," said he, as she came to it.

Amaryllis did so, and said that the coins and medals in it were very interesting, as they really were. The smoke caught her in the throat, and seemed to stop the air as she breathed from reaching her chest. So much accustomed to the open air, she felt stifled.

Then he asked her to read to him aloud, that he might hear how she enunciated her words. The book he gave her was an early copy of Addison, the page a pale yellow, the type old-fount, the edges rough, but where in a trim modern volume will you find language like his and ideas set forth with such transparent lucidity? How easy to write like that!—so simple, merely a letter to an intimate friend; but try!

Trim modern volumes are so very hard to read, especially those that come to us from New York, thick volumes of several hundred pages, printed on the thinnest paper in hard, unpleasant type. You cannot read them; you work through them.

The French have retained a little of the old style of book in their paper bound franc novels, the rough paper, thick black type, rough edges are pleasant to touch and look at—they feel as if they were done by hand, not turned out hurriedly smooth and trim by machinery.

Docile to the last degree with him, Amaryllis tried her utmost to read well, and she succeeded, so far as the choking smoke would let her. By grunting between his continuous fits of coughing the old man signified his approval.

Amaryllis would have been respectful to any of the aged, but she had a motive here; she wanted to please him for her father's sake. For many years there had been an increasing estrangement between the younger and the elder Iden; an estrangement which no one could have explained, for it could hardly be due to money matters if Grandfather Iden was really so rich. The son was his father's tenant—the farm belonged to Grandfather Iden—and perhaps the rent was not paid regularly. Still that could not have much mattered—a mere trifle to a man of old Iden's wealth. There was something behind, no one knew what; possibly they scarcely knew themselves, for it is a fact that people frequently fall into a quarrel without remembering the beginning.

Amaryllis was very anxious to please the old man for her father's sake; her dear father, whom she loved so much. Tradesmen were for ever worrying him for petty sums of money; it made her furious with indignation to see and hear it.

So she read her very best, and swallowed the choking smoke patiently.

Among the yellow pages, pressed flat, and still as fresh as if gathered yesterday, Amaryllis found bright petals and coloured autumn leaves. For it was one of the old man's ways to carry home such of these that pleased him and to place them in his books. This he had done for half a century, and many of the flower petals and leaves in the grey old works of bygone authors had been there a generation. It is wonderful how long they will endure left undisturbed and pressed in this way; the paper they used in old books seems to have been softer, without the hard surface of our present paper, more like blotting paper, and so keeps them better. Before the repulsion between father and son became so marked, Amaryllis had often been with her grandfather in the garden and round the meadows at Coombe Oaks, and seen him gather the yellow tulips, the broad-petalled roses, and in autumn the bright scarlet bramble leaves. The brown leaves of the Spanish chestnut, too, pleased him; anything with richness of colour. The old and grey, and withered man gathered the brightest of petals for his old and grey, and forgotten books.

Now the sight of these leaves and petals between the yellow pages softened her heart towards him; he was a tyrant, but he was very, very old, they were like flowers on a living tomb.

In a little while Grandfather Iden got up, and going to a drawer in one of the bookcases, took from it some scraps of memoranda; he thrust these between her face and the book, and told her to read them instead.

"These are your writing."

"Go on," said the old man, smiling, grunting, and coughing, all at once.

"In 1840," read Amaryllis, "there were only two houses in Black Jack Street." "Only two houses!" she interposed, artfully.

"Two," said the grandfather.

"One in 1802," went on Amaryllis, "while in 1775 the site was covered with furze." "How it has changed!" she said. He nodded, and coughed, and smiled; his great grey hat rocked on his head and seemed about to extinguish him.

"There's a note at the bottom in pencil, grandpa. It says, 'A hundred voters in this street, 1884.'"

"Ah!" said the old man, an ah! so deep it fetched his very heart up in coughing. When he finished, Amaryllis read on—

"In 1802 there were only ten voters in the town."

"Ah!" His excitement caused such violent coughing Amaryllis became alarmed, but it did him no harm. The more he coughed and choked the livelier he seemed. The thought of politics roused him like a trumpet—it went straight to his ancient heart.

"Read that again," he said. "How many voters now?"

"A hundred voters in this street, 1884."

"We've got them all"—coughing—"all in my lord's houses, everyone; vote Conservative, one and all. What is it?" as some one knocked. Dinner was ready, to Amaryllis's relief.

"Perhaps you would like to dine with me?" asked the

grandfather, shuffling up his papers. "There—there," as she hesitated, "you would like to dine with young people, of course—of course."

CHAPTER XII

OLD Grandfather Iden always dined alone in the parlour, with his housekeeper to wait on him; they were just bringing in his food. The family and visitors had their meals in a separate and much more comfortable apartment in another part of the house, which was large. Sometimes, as a great favour and special mark of approval, the old Pacha would invite you to eat with him.

Amaryllis, though anxious to please him, hesitated, not only because of the smoke, but because she knew he always had pork for dinner.

The rich juices of roast pork sustained his dry and withered frame—it was a sort of Burgundy of flesh to him. As the good wine of Burgundy fills the blood with iron and strengthens the body, so the rich juice of the pork seemed to supply the oil necessary to keep the sinews supple and to prevent the cartilages from stiffening.

The scientific people say that it is the ossification of the cartilages—the stiffening of the firmer tissues—that in time interferes with the processes of life. The hinges rust, as if your tricycle had been left out in the rain for a week—and the delicate watchwork of the human frame will not run.

If suppleness could only be maintained there is no reason why it should not continue to work for a much longer period, for a hundred and fifty, two hundred years—as long as you fancy. But nothing has yet been devised to keep up the suppleness.

Grandfather Iden found the elixir of life in roast pork. The jokers of Woolhorton—there are always jokers, very clever they think themselves—considered the reason it suited him so well was because of the pig-like obstinacy of his disposition.

Anything more contrary to common sense than for an old man of ninety to feed on pork it would be hard to discover—so his friends said.

"Pork," said the physician, had down from London to see him

on one occasion, "pork is the first on the list of indigestible articles of food. It takes from six to eight hours for the gastric apparatus to reduce its fibres. The stomach becomes overloaded—acidity is the result; nightmares, pains, and innumerable ills are the consequence. The very worst thing Mr. Iden could eat."

"Hum," growled the family doctor, a native of Woolhorton, when he heard of this. "Hum!" low in his throat, like an irate bulldog. If in the least excited, like most other country folk, he used the provincial pronunciation. "Hum! A' have lived twenty years on pork. Let'n yet it!"

Grandfather Iden intended to eat it, and did eat it six days out of seven, not, of course, roast pork every dinner; sometimes boiled pork; sometimes he baked it himself in the great oven. Now and then he varied it with pig-meat—good old country meat, let me tell you, pig-meat—such as spare-rib, griskin, blade-bone, and that mysterious morsel, the "mouse." The chine he always sent over for Iden junior, who was a chine eater—a true Homeric diner—and to make it even, Iden junior sent in the best apples for sauce from his favourite russet trees. It was about the only amenity that survived between father and son.

The pig-meat used to be delicious in the old house at home, before we all went astray along the different paths of life; fresh from the pigs fed and killed on the premises, nutty, and juicy to the palate. Much of it is best done on a gridiron—here's heresy! A gridiron is flat blasphemy to the modern school of scientific cookery. Scientific fiddlestick! Nothing like a gridiron to set your lips watering.

But the "mouse,"—what was the "mouse?" The London butchers can't tell me. It was a titbit. I suppose it still exists in pigs; but London folk are so ignorant.

Grandfather Iden ate pig in every shape and form, that is, he mumbled the juice out of it, and never complained of indigestion.

He was up at five o'clock every morning of his life, pottering about the great oven with his baker's man. In summer if it was fine he went out at six for a walk in the Pines—the promenade of Woolhorton.

"If you wants to get well," old Dr. Butler used to say, "you go for a walk in the marning afore the aair have been braathed auver."

Before the air has been breathed over—inspired and re-inspired by human crowds, while it retains the sweetness of the morning, like water fresh from the spring; that was when it possessed its value, according to bluff, gruff, rule-of-thumb old Butler. Depend upon it, there is something in his dictum, too.

Amaryllis hesitated at the thought of the pork, for he often

49

had it underdone, so the old gentleman dismissed her in his most gracious manner to dine with the rest.

She went down the corridor and took the seat placed for her. There was a posy of primroses beside her napkin—posies of primroses all round the table.

This raging old Tory of ninety years would give a shilling for the earliest primrose the boys could find for him in the woods. Some one got him a peacock's feather which had fallen from Beaconsfield's favourites—a real Beaconsfield peacock-feather— which he had set in the centre of a splendid screen of feathers that cost him twenty guineas. The screen was upstairs in the great drawing-room near a bow window which overlooked the fair.

People, you see, took pains to get him feathers and anything he fancied, on account of the twenty thousand spade guineas in the iron box under the bed.

His daughters, elderly, uninteresting married folk, begged him not to keep a peacock's feather in the house—it would certainly bring misfortune. The superstition was so firmly rooted in their minds that they actually argued with him—argued with Grandfather Iden!—pointing out to him the fearful risk he was running. He puffed and coughed, and grew red in the face—the great grey hat shook and tottered with anger; not for all the Powers of Darkness would he have given up that feather.

The chairs round the large table were arranged in accordance with the age of the occupants. There were twenty-one grandchildren, and a number of aunts, uncles, and so on; a vague crowd that does not concern us. The eldest sat at the head of the table, the next in age followed, and so all round the dishes. This arrangement placed Amaryllis rather low down—a long way from the top and fountain of honour—and highly displeased her. She despised and disliked the whole vague crowd of her relations, yet being there, she felt that she ought to have had a position above them all. Her father—Iden, junior—was old Iden's only son and natural heir; therefore her father's chair ought to have been at the top of the table, and hers ought to have been next to his.

Instead of which, as her father was not the eldest, his seat was some distance from the top, and hers again, was a long way from his.

All the other chairs were full, but her father's chair was empty.

The vague crowd were so immensely eager to pay their despicable court to the Spade-Guinea Man, not one of them stopped away; the old, the young, the lame, the paralytic, all found means to creep in to Grandfather Iden's annual dinner. His only son and natural heir was alone absent. How eagerly poor Amaryllis glanced from time to time at that empty chair, hoping against hope that her dear father would come in at the Psalms, or even at the sermon, and disappoint the venomous, avaricious hearts of the enemies around her.

For well she knew how delighted they were to see his chair empty, as a visible sign and token of the gulf between father and son, and well she knew how diligently each laboured to deepen the misunderstanding and set fuel to the flame of the quarrel. If the son were disinherited, consider the enormous profit to the rest of them!

Grandfather Iden made no secret of the fact that he had not signed a will. It was believed that several rough drafts had been sketched out for him, but, in his own words—and he was no teller of falsehoods—he had not decided on his will. If only they could persuade him to make his will they might feel safe of something; but suppose he went off pop, all in a moment, as these extraordinarily healthy old people are said to do, and the most of his estate in land! Consider what a contingency—almost all of it would go to his own son. Awful thing!

Amaryllis was aware how they all stared at her and quizzed her over and over; her hair, her face, her form, but most of all her dress. They were so poor at home she had not had a new dress this twelvemonth past; it was true her dress was decent and comfortable, and she really looked very nice in it to any man's eye; but a girl does not want a comfortable dress, she wants something in the style of the day, and just sufficiently advanced to make the women's eyes turn green with envy. It is not the men's eyes; it is the women's eyes.

Amaryllis sat up very quiet and unconcerned, trying with all her might to make them feel she was the Heiress, not only an only son's only daughter, but the only son's only offspring—doubly the Heiress of Grandfather Iden.

The old folk, curious in such matters, had prophesied so soon as she was born that there would be no more children at Coombe Oaks, and so it fell out. For it had been noticed in the course of generations, that in the direct line of Iden when the first child was a daughter there were none to follow. And further, that there never was but one Miss Iden at a time.

If the Direct Line had a daughter first, they never had any more children; consequently that daughter was the only Miss Iden.

If the Direct Line had a son, they never had a second son, though they might have daughters; but then, in order that there should still be only one Miss Iden, it always happened that the first died, or was married early, before the second came into existence.

Such was the tradition of the Iden family; they had a long

pedigree, the Idens, reaching farther back than the genealogies of many a peer, and it had been observed that this was the rule of their descent.

Amaryllis was the only Miss Iden, and the heiress, through her father, of the Spade-Guinea Man. She tried to make them feel that she knew it and felt it; that she was the Iden of the Idens. Her proud face—it was a very proud face naturally—darkened a little, and grew still more disdainful in its utter scorn and loathing of the vague crowd of enemies.

CHAPTER XIII

TO one, as it were, in the gallery, it was a delight to see her; her sweet cheeks, fresh as the dawn, reddening with suppressed indignation; her young brow bent; her eyes cast down—don't you think for a moment she would deign to look at them—pride in her heart, and resolute determination to fight for her dear father and mother.

But she felt as she sat so unconcerned that there was a crack in her boot unmended, and it seemed as if everyone could see it though under the solid table. She had not had a really sound pair of boots for many, many months; they could not afford her a new pair at home, and the stupid shoemaker, "Established 1697," was such a time repairing her others.

She would not look at them, but she knew that they were all dressed better than she was; there were some of them very poor, and very vulgar, too, but they were all dressed better than her, and without a doubt had sound boots on their feet.

The cottagers in Coombe hamlet always had sound boots; she never had; nor, indeed, her mother. Her father had a pair, being compelled by the character of his work in the fields to take care of himself so far, though he wore a ragged coat. But neither mother nor daughter ever had a whole pair of boots—whole and sound as the very cottagers had.

If Amaryllis had sat there with naked feet she would have been prouder than ever, and that is why I always loved her so; she was not to be put down by circumstances, she was above external things.

But as time went on, and the dinner was nearly over—she had scarcely eaten anything—and as she glanced from time to time at her father's empty chair, and knew that he would not come, and that his defection would revive the old quarrel which might so easily have been mended, the Flamma blood began to rise and grow hotter and hotter, and the foot with the worn boot on it began to tap the floor.

The Flamma blood would have liked to have swept the whole company over a precipice into the Red Sea as the herd of swine in old time. It was either the Red Sea or somewhere; geography is of no consequence.

> Spain's an island near
> Morocco, betwixt Egypt and Tangier.

The Flamma blood would have liked to have seen them all poisoned and dying on their seats.

The Flamma blood would have been glad to stick a knife into each of them—only it would not have touched them with the longest hop-pole in Kent, so utter was its loathing of the crew gloating over that empty chair.

And for once Amaryllis did not check it, and did not say to herself, "I will not be a Flamma."

Towards the end of the tedious banquet the word was passed round that everyone was to sit still, as Grandfather Iden was coming to look at his descendants.

There was not the least fear of any of them stirring, for they well knew his custom—to walk round, and speak a few words to everyone in turn, and to put a new golden sovereign into their hands. Thirty-two sovereigns it was in all—one for each—but the thirty-third was always a spade-guinea, which was presented to the individual who had best pleased him during the year.

A genial sort of custom, no doubt, but fancy the emulation and the heart-burning over the spade-guinea! For the fortunate winner usually considered himself the nearest to the Will.

Amaryllis' cheeks began to burn at the thought that she should have to take his horrible money. A hideous old monster he was to her at that moment—not that he had done anything to her personally—but he left her dear father to be worried out of his life by petty tradesmen, and her dear mother to go without a pair of decent boots, while he made this pompous distribution among these wretches. The hideous old monster!

53

Out in the town the boys behind his back gave him endless nicknames: Granfer Iden, Floury Iden, My Lord Lardy-Cake, Marquis Iden, His Greasy Grace; and, indeed, with his whims and humours, and patronage, his caprices and ways of going on, if he had but had a patent of nobility, Grandfather Iden would have made a wonderfully good duke.

By-and-by in comes the old Pacha, still wearing his great grey tottery hat, and proceeds from chair to chair, tapping folk on the shoulder, saying a gracious word or two, and dropping his new golden sovereigns in their eager palms. There was a loud hum of conversation as he went round; they all tried to appear so immensely happy to see him.

Amaryllis did not exactly watch him, but of course knew what he was about, when suddenly there was a dead silence. Thirty-two people suddenly stopped talking as if the pneumatic brake had been applied to their lips by a sixty-ton locomotive.

Dead, ominous silence. You could almost hear the cat licking his paw under the table.

Amaryllis looked, and saw the old man leaning with both hands on the back of his son's empty chair.

He seemed to cling to it as if it was a spar floating on the barren ocean of life and death into which his withered old body was sinking.

Perhaps he really would have clung like that to his son had but his son come to him, and borne a little, and for a little while, with his ways.

A sorrowful thing to see—the old man of ninety clinging to the back of his son's empty chair. His great grey tottery hat seemed about to tumble on the floor—his back bowed a little more—and he groaned deeply, three times.

We can see, being out of the play and spectators merely, that there was a human cry for help in the old man's groan—his heart yearned for his son's strong arm to lean on.

The crowd of relations were in doubt as to whether they should rejoice, whether the groan was a sign of indignation, of anger too deep ever to be forgotten, or whether they should be alarmed at the possibility of reconciliation.

The Flamma blood was up too much in Amaryllis for her to feel pity for him as she would have done in any other mood; she hated him all the more; he was rich, the five-shilling fare was nothing to him, he could hire a fly from the "Lamb Inn," and drive over and make friends with her father in half an hour. Groaning there—the hideous old monster! and her mother without a decent pair of boots.

In a moment or two Grandfather Iden recovered himself, and continued the distribution, and by-and-by Amaryllis felt him approach her chair. She did not even turn to look at him, so he took her hand, and placed two coins in it, saying in his most gracious way that the sovereign was for her father, and the guinea—the spade-guinea—for herself. She muttered something—she knew not what—she could but just restrain herself from throwing the money on the floor.

It was known in a moment that Amaryllis had the guinea. Conceive the horror, the hatred, the dread of the crowd of sycophants! That the Heiress Apparent should be the favourite!

Yet more. Half-an-hour later, just after they had all got upstairs into the great drawing-room, and some were officiously and reverently admiring the peacock-feather in the screen, and some looking out of the bow window at the fair, there came a message for Amaryllis to put on her hat and go for a walk with her grandfather.

There was not one among all the crowd in the drawing-room who had ever been invited to accompany Iden Pacha.

Three days ago at home, if anyone had told Amaryllis that she would be singled out in this way, first to receive the Iden medal—the spade-guinea stamp of approval—and then, above all things, to be honoured by walking out with this "almighty" grandfather, how delighted she would have been at the thought of the triumph!

But now it was just the reverse. Triumph over these people—pah! a triumph over rats and flies or some such creatures. She actually felt lowered in her own esteem by being noticed at all among them. Honoured by this old horror—she revolted at it. He honour her with his approval—she hated him.

The other day a travelling piano was wheeled through Coombe and set up a tune in that lonesome spot. Though it was but a mechanical piece of music, with the cogs as it were of the mechanism well marked by the thump, thump, it seemed to cheer the place—till she went out to the gate to look at the Italian woman who danced about while the grinding was done, and saw that she had a sound pair of boots on. That very morning her mother in crossing the road had set the Flamma rheumatism shooting in her bones, for the dampness of the mud came through the crack in her boot.

This miserable old Iden Pacha thought to honour her while he let her mother walk about with her stocking on the wet ground!

The Flamma blood was up in her veins—what did she care for guineas!

As she was putting her hat on in the bedroom before the glass she looked round to see that no one was watching, and then stooped down and put the spade-guinea in the dust of the floor under the dressing-table. She would have none of his hateful money. The sovereign she took care of because it was for her father, and he might buy something useful with it; he wanted a few shillings badly enough.

So the spade-guinea remained in the dust of the floor for a week or two, till it pleased the housemaid to move the dressing-table to brush away the accumulation, when she found the shining one in the fluff.

Being over thirty, she held her tongue, the guinea henceforward travelled down the stream of Time fast enough though silently, but she took the first opportunity of examining the iron box under the Pacha's bed, thinking perhaps there might be a chink in it. And it was curious how for some time afterwards a fit of extraordinary industry prevailed in the house; there was not a table, a chair, or any piece of furniture that was not chivvied about under pretence of polishing. She actually had a day's holiday and a cast-off gown given to her as a reward for her labours.

CHAPTER XIV

AMARYLLIS did not look back as she walked beside her grandfather slowly up the street, or she would have seen the company of relations watching them from the bow-window.

Iden went straight through the crowd without any hesitation on account of his age—angry as she was, Amaryllis feared several times lest the clumsy people should over-turn him, and tried her best to shield him. But he had a knack of keeping on his feet—the sort of knack you learn by skating—and did not totter much more than usual, despite the press.

The world gets on with very little amusement somehow. Here were two or three thousand people packed in the street, and all they had to enliven their festive gathering was the same old toys their fathers' fathers' fathers had set before them.

Rows of booths for the display of "fairings," gingerbread, nuts, cakes, brandy-balls, and sugar-plums stood in the gutter each side.

56

The "fairings" were sweet biscuits—they have been made every fair this hundred years.

The nuts were dry and hard, just as Spanish nuts always are. The gingerbread was moulded in the same old shapes of clumsy horses outlined with gilt.

There was the same old trumpeting and tootling, tom-tomming, and roaring of showmen's voices. The same old roundabouts, only now they were driven by steam, and short, quick whistles announced that the whirligig caravan was travelling round the world. The fat woman, the strong man, the smashers tapping the "claret," the "Pelican of the Wilderness," that mystic and melancholy bird, the rifle galleries, the popping for nuts—behold these are they our fathers have seen.

There is nothing new under the sun—not even at Epsom. The first time I saw the wonderful crowd of the Derby Day—perhaps the largest crowd in the world—I could scarcely believe my eyes, for I found on passing through it that the hundreds of thousands of people there had nothing more to amuse them than they would have found at an ordinary country fair. Swings, roundabouts, cockshies at cocoa-nuts, rootletum, tootletum, and beer. That was all. No new amusement whatsoever: a very humdrum sort of world, my masters!

The next finest crowd is the crowd on August bank-holiday all along the Brighton beach, and there it is just the same. Nothing for the folk but Punch, brass bands, and somersaulters—dull old stories in my grandmother's time.

Xerxes offered a reward to anyone who could invent him a fresh pleasure—the multitude of the Derby Day and Brighton beach should do the same. But indeed they do, for an immense fortune would certainly be the reward of such a discoverer. One gets tired of pitching sticks at cocoa-nuts all one's time.

However, at Woolhorton nobody but the very rawest and crudest folk cared for the shows, all they did care was to alternately stand stock still and then shove. First they shoved as far as the "Lion" and had some beer, then they shoved back to the "Lamb" and had some beer, then they stood stock still in the street and blocked those who were shoving. Several thousand people were thus happily occupied, and the Lion and the Lamb laid down together peacefully that day.

Amaryllis and old Iden had in like manner to shove, for there was no other way to get through, no one thought of moving, or giving any passage, if you wanted to progress you must shoulder them aside. As Grandfather Iden could not shove very hard they were frequently compelled to wait till the groups opened, and thus it happened that Amaryllis found herself once face to face with Jack Duck.

He kind of sniggered in a foolish way at Amaryllis, and touched his hat to Iden. "You ain't a been over to Coombe lately, Mr. Iden," he said.

"No," replied the old man sharply, and went on.

Jack could hardly have struck a note more discordant to Amaryllis. The father had not been to visit his son for more than a year—she did not want unpleasant memories stirred up.

Again in another group a sturdy labourer touched his hat and asked her if her father was at fair, as he was looking out for a job. Old Iden started and grunted like a snorting horse.

Amaryllis, though put out, stayed to speak kindly to him, for she knew he was always in difficulties. Bill Nye was that contradiction a strong man without work. He wanted to engage for mowing. Bill Nye was a mower at Coombe, and his father, Bill Nye, before him, many a long year before he was discovered in California.

When she overtook Iden he was struggling to pass the stream of the Orinoco, which set strongly at that moment out of the "Lamb" towards the "Lion." Strong men pushed out from the "Lamb" archway like a river into the sea, thrusting their way into the general crowd, and this mighty current cast back the tottering figure of old Iden as the swollen Orinoco swung the crank old Spanish caravels that tried to breast it.

It was as much as Amaryllis and he together could do to hold their ground at the edge of the current. While they were thus battling she chanced to look up.

A large window was open over the archway, and at this window a fellow was staring down at her. He stood in his shirt-sleeves with a billiard-cue in his hand waiting his turn to play. It was the same young fellow, gentleman if you like, whose pale face had so displeased her that morning as he rode under when she watched the folk go by to fair. He was certainly the most advanced in civilization of all who had passed Plum Corner, and yet there was something in that pale and rather delicate face which was not in the coarse lineaments of the "varmers" and "drauvers" and "pig-dealers" who had gone by under the wall. Something that insulted her.

The face at the window was appraising her.

It was reckoning her up—so much for eyes, so much for hair, so much for figure, and as this went on the fingers were filling a pipe from an elastic tobacco-pouch. There was no romance, no poetry in that calculation—no rapture or pure admiration of beauty; there was a billiard-cue and a tobacco-pouch, and a glass of spirits and water, and an atmosphere of smoke, and a sound of clicking ivory balls at the back of the thought. His thumb was white where he had chalked it to make a better bridge for the cue. His face was white; for he had chalked it with dissipation. His physical body was whitened—chalked—a whited sepulchre; his moral nature likewise chalked.

At the back of his thought lay not the high esteem of the poet-thinker for beauty, but the cynical blackguardism of the XIXth century.

The cynicism that deliberately reckons up things a Shakespeare would admire at their lowest possible sale value. A slow whiff of smoke from a corner of the sneering mouth, an air of intense knowingness, as much as to say, "You may depend upon me—I've been behind the scenes. All this is got up, you know; stage effect in front, pasteboard at the rear; nothing in it."

In the sensuality of Nero there may still be found some trace of a higher nature; "What an artist the world has lost!" he exclaimed, dying.

The empress Theodora craved for the applause of the theatre to which she exposed her beauty.

This low, cynical nineteenth century blackguardism thinks of nothing but lowness, and has no ideal. The milliner even has an ideal, she looks to colour, shape, effect; though but in dress, yet it is an ideal. There was no ideal in Ned Marks.

They called him from within to take his turn with the cue; he did not answer, he was so absorbed in his calculations. He was clever—in a way; he had quite sufficient penetration to see that this was no common girl. She was not beautiful—yet, she was not even pretty, and so plainly dressed; still there was something marked in her features. And she was with old Iden.

Amaryllis did not understand the meaning of his glance, but she felt that it was an insult. She looked down quickly, seized her grandfather's arm, and drew him out from the pavement into the street, yielding a little to the current and so hoping to presently pass it.

By this time, as Ned Marks did not answer, his companions had come to the window to discover what he was staring at. "Oho!" they laughed. "It's Miss Iden. Twenty thousand guineas in the iron box!"

Iden's great white hat, which always seemed to sit loosely on his head, was knocked aside by the elbow of a burly butcher struggling in the throng; Amaryllis replaced it upright, and leading him this way, and pushing him that, got at last to the opposite pavement, and so behind the row of booths, between them and the houses where there was less crush. Taking care of him, she forgot to look to her feet and stepped in the gutter where there was a puddle. The cold water came through the crack in her boot.

While these incidents were still further irritating her, the old Pacha kept mumbling and muttering to himself, nodding his head and smiling at each fresh mark of attention, for though he was so independent and fearless still he appreciated the trouble she took. The mumbling in his mouth was a sort of purring. Her dutiful spirit had stroked him up to a pleasant state of electric glow; she felt like a hound in a leash, ready to burst the bond that held her to his hand. Side by side, and arm in arm, neither of them understood the other: ninety and sixteen, a strange couple in the jostling fair.

Iden turned down a passage near the end of the street, and in an instant the roar of the crowd which had boomed all round them was shut off by high walls up which it rose and hummed over their heads in the air. They walked on broad stone flags notched here and there at the edges, for the rest worn smooth by footsteps (the grave drives such a trade) like Iden's doorstep, they were in fact tombstones, and the walled passage brought them to the porch of the Abbey church.

There he stopped, muttering and mumbling, and wiped his forehead with his vast silk handkerchief. They were no longer incommoded by a crowd, but now and then folk came by hastening to the fair; lads with favours in their coats, and blue ribbons in their hats, girls in bright dresses, chiefly crude colours, who seemed out of accord with the heavy weight as it were of the great Abbey, the ponderous walls, the quiet gloom of the narrow space, and the shadows that lurked behind the buttresses.

The aged man muttered and mumbled about the porch and took Amaryllis under it, making her look up at the groining, and note the spring of the arch, which formed a sort of carved crown over them. It was a fine old porch, deep and high, in some things reminding you of the porches that are to be seen in Spain; stone made to give a pleasant shade like trees, so cut and worked as to be soft to the eye.

He pointed out to her the touches that rendered it so dear to those who value art in stone. He knew them, every one, the history and the dates, and the three stags' heads on a shield; there were broad folios in the smoky room at home, filled with every detail, Iden himself had subscribed forty pounds to the cost of illustrating one of them. Every scholar who visited the Abbey church, called and begged to see the baker's old books.

Iden rubbed his old thumb in the grooves and went outside and hoisted himself, as it were, up from his crooked S position to look at the three stags' heads on the shield on the wall; dim stags' heads that to you, or at least to me, might have been fishes, or Jove's thunderbolts, or anything.

Amaryllis was left standing alone a moment in the porch, the deep shadow within behind her, the curve of the arch over, a fine setting for a portrait. She stood the more upright because of the fire and temper suppressed in her.

Just outside the human letter S—crooked S—clad in sad white-grey miller's garments, its old hat almost falling backwards off its old grey head, gazed up and pointed with its oaken cudgel at the coat of arms. Seven hundred years—the weight of seven hundred years—hung over them both in that old Abbey.

Into that Past he was soon to disappear: she came out to the Future.

Thence he took her to an arched door, nail-studded, in the passage wall, and giving her the key, told her to open it, and stood watching her in triumph, as if it had been the door to some immense treasury. She turned the lock, and he pushed her before him hastily, as if they must snatch so grand an opportunity.

CHAPTER XV

WITHIN there was a gravel path, and glimpses between trees of wide pleasure-grounds. Amaryllis hesitated, and looked back; Iden drew her forward, not noticing her evident disinclination to proceed. If he had, he would have put it down to awe, instead of which it was dislike.

For she guessed they were entering the lawns in front of the Hon. Raleigh Pamment's mansion. He was the largest owner of town and country; the streets, the market-place, the open spaces, in which the fair was being held, belonged to him; so did most of the farms and hamlets out of which the people had come. The Pamments were Tories; very important Tories indeed.

The Idens, in their little way, were Tories, too, right to the centre of the cerebellum; the Flammas were hot Republicans. Now Amaryllis, being a girl, naturally loved her father most, yet she was a wilful and rebellious revolutionist. Amaryllis, who would not be a

61

Flamma, had imbibed all the Flamma hatred of authority from her mother.

To her the Pamments were the incarnation of everything detestable, of oppression, obstruction, and mediæval darkness. She knew nothing of politics; at sixteen you do not need to know to feel vehemently, you feel vehemently without knowing. Still, she had heard a good deal about the Pamments.

She resented being brought there to admire the pleasure grounds and mansion, and to kow-tow to the grandeur of these mediæval tyrants.

Old Iden led her on till they came to the smooth lawn before the front windows; three centuries of mowing had made it as smooth as the top of his own head, where the years had mown away merrily.

There was not so much as a shrub—not a daisy—between them and the great windows of the house. They stood in full view.

Amaryllis could scarcely endure herself, so keen was her vexation; her cheeks reddened. She was obliged to face the house, but her glance was downwards; she would not look at it.

Grandfather Iden was in the height of his glory. In all Woolhorton town there was not another man who could do as he was doing at that moment.

The Pamments were very exclusive people, exceptionally exclusive even for high class Tories. Their gardens, and lawns, and grounds were jealously surrounded with walls higher than the old-fashioned houses of the street beneath them. No one dared to so much as peer through a crevice of the mighty gates. Their persons were encircled with the "divinity" that hedges the omnipotent landed proprietor. No one dared speak to a Pamment. They acknowledged no one in the town, not even the solicitors, not even the clergyman of the Abbey church; that was on account of ritual differences.

It was, indeed, whispered—high treason must always be whispered—that young Pamment, the son and heir, was by no means so exclusive, and had been known to be effusive towards ladies of low birth—and manners.

The great leaders of Greece—Alcibiades, Aristides, and so on—threw open their orchards to the people. Everyone walked in and did as he chose. These great leaders of England—the Pamments—shut up their lawns and pleasure-grounds, sealed them hermetically, you could hardly throw a stone over the walls if you tried.

But Grandfather Iden walked through those walls as if there were none; he alone of all Woolhorton town and country.

In that gossipy little town, of course, there were endless surmises as to the why and wherefore of that private key. Shrewd people said—"Ah! you may depend they be getting summat out of him. Lent 'em some of his guineas, a' reckon. They be getting summat out of him. Hoss-leeches, they gentlefolks."

Grandfather Iden alone entered when he listed: he wandered about the lawns, he looked in at the conservatories, he took a bunch of grapes if it pleased him, or a bouquet of flowers; he actually stepped indoors occasionally and sat down on the carved old chairs, or pottered about the picture gallery. He had a private key to the nail-studded door in the wall by the Abbey church, and he looked upon that key very much as if it had been the key of Paradise.

When Grandfather Iden stood on the lawn at Pamment House he was the proudest and happiest man in what they sarcastically call "God's creation."

He was a peer at such moments; a grandee—the grandee who can wear his hat or sit down (which is it? it is most important to be accurate) in the presence of his deity, I mean his sovereign; he could actually step on the same sward pressed by the holy toes of the Pamments.

In justice to him it must be said that he was most careful not to obtrude himself into the sight of their sacred majesties. If they were at home he rarely went in, if he did he crept round unfrequented paths, the byeways of the gardens, and hid himself under the fig trees, as it were. But if by chance a Pamment did light upon him, it was noteworthy that he was literally dandled and fondled like an infant, begged to come in, and take wine, and so so, and so so.

In justice to old Iden let it be known that he was most careful not to obtrude himself; he hid himself under the fig trees.

Hardly credible is it? that a man of ninety years—a man of no common intelligence—a man of books, and coins, and antiquities, should, in this nineteenth century, bend his aged knees in such a worship. Incredible as it may seem it is certainly true.

Such loyalty in others of old time, remember, seems very beautiful when we read of the devotion that was shown towards Charles Stuart.

With all his heart and soul he worshipped the very ground the Pamments trod on. He loved to see them in the Abbey church; when they were at home he never failed to attend service, rain, snow, thunder, ninety years notwithstanding, he always attended that he might bow his venerable head to them as they swept up the aisle, receiving the faintest, yet most gracious, smile of recognition in return.

He was quite happy in his pew if he could see them at their carved desks in the chancel; the organ sounded very beautiful then; the light came sweetly through the painted windows; a sanctity and heavenly presence was diffused around.

Rebellious Amaryllis knew all this, and hated it. Her Flamma foot tapped the sacred sward.

Grandfather Iden, after mopping his mouth with his silk handkerchief, began to point with his cudgel—a big hockey stick—at the various parts of the building. This was Elizabethan, that dated from James II., that went back to Henry VII., there were walls and foundations far more ancient still, out of sight.

Really, it was a very interesting place archæologically, if only you could have got rid of the Pamments.

Amaryllis made no remark during this mumbling history. Iden thought she was listening intently. At the conclusion he was just moving her—for she was passive now, like a piece of furniture—when he spied some one at a window.

Off came the great white hat, and down it swept till the top brushed the grass in the depth of his homage. It was a bow that would have delighted a lady, so evidently real in its intent, so full of the gentleman, so thoroughly courtier-like, and yet honest. There was nothing to smile at in that bow; there was not a young gentleman in Belgravia who could bow in that way, for, in truth, we have forgotten how to bow in this generation.

A writing and talking is always going on about the high place woman occupies in modern society, but the fact is, we have lost our reverence for woman as woman; it is after-dinner speech, nothing more, mere sham. We don't venerate woman, and therefore we don't bow.

Grandfather Iden's bow would have won any woman's heart had it been addressed to her, for there was veneration and courtesy, breeding, and desire to please in it.

CHAPTER XVI

THE man he had seen at the window was young Raleigh Pamment, the son and heir.

He had been sitting in an easy chair, one leg over the arm, busy with a memorandum book, a stump of pencil, and a disordered heap of telegrams, letters, and newspapers.

Everybody writes to Mr. Gladstone, a sort of human lion's mouth for post-cards, but Raleigh junior had not got to manage the House of Commons, the revenue, the nation, the Turks, South Africa, the Nile, Ganges, Indus, Afghanistan, sugar, shipping, and Homer.

Yet Raleigh junior had an occasional table beside him, from which the letters, telegrams, newspapers, and scraps of paper had overflowed on to the floor. In a company's offices it would have taken sixteen clerks to answer that correspondence; this idle young aristocrat answered it himself, entered it in his day book, "totted" it up, and balanced the—the residue.

Nothing at all businesslike, either, about him—nothing in the least like those gentlemen who consider that to go in to the "office" every morning is the sum total of life. A most unbusinesslike young fellow.

A clay pipe in his mouth, a jar of tobacco on another chair beside him, a glass of whiskey for a paper-weight on his telegrams. An idle, lounging, "bad lot;" late hours, tobacco, whiskey, and ballet-dancers writ very large indeed on his broad face. In short, a young "gent" of the latter half of the nineteenth century.

Not the slightest sign of "blue blood" anywhere; not even in the cut of his coat, no Brummel-like elegance; hardly a Bond Street coat at all—rough, large, coarse cloth. If he had stood at the door of a shop he would have done very well indeed for a shopkeeper, the sort that drives about in a cart for orders.

Of his character nothing could be learned from his features. His face was broad, rather flat, with a short but prominent nose; in spite of indulgence, he kept a good, healthy, country colour. His neck was thick, his figure stout, his hands big—a jovial, good-tempered looking man.

His neck was very thick, tree-like; a drover's neck, no refinement or special intelligence indicated there; great power to eat, drink, and sleep—belly energy.

But let no one, therefore, suppose that the members of the

upper ten thousand are any thicker in the neck, or more abdominal in their proclivities, or beneath the culture of the day. Take five hundred "blue bloods," and you will find among them a certain proportion of thick-necked people; take five hundred very common commoners, and you may count exactly the same number interspersed.

The Pamments were simply Englishmen, and liable to be born big, with broad faces, thick necks, and ultimate livers. It was no disgrace to Raleigh, that jolly neck of his.

Unless you are given to æsthetic crockery, or Francesco de Rimini, I think you would rather have liked him; a sort of fellow who would lend you his dogs, or his gun, or his horse, or his ballet-dancer, or his credit—humph!—at a moment's notice. But he was a very "bad lot;" they whispered it even in dutiful Woolhorton.

He got rid of money in a most surprising way, and naturally had nothing to show for it. The wonderful manner in which coin will disappear in London, like water into deep sand, surpasses the mysteries of the skies. It slips, it slides, it glides, it sinks, it flies, it runs out of the pocket. The nimble squirrel is nothing to the way in which a sovereign will leap forth in town.

Raleigh had a good allowance, often supplemented by soft aunts, yet he frequently walked for lack of a cab fare. I can't blame him; I should be just as bad, if fortune favoured me. How delicious now to walk down Regent Street, along Piccadilly, up Bond Street, and so on, in a widening circle, with a thousand pounds in one's pocket, just to spend, all your own, and no need to worry when it was gone. To look in at all the shops and pick up something here and something yonder, to say, "I'll have that picture I admired ten years ago; I'll have a bit of real old oak furniture; I'll go to Paris—" but Paris is not a patch on London. To take a lady—the lady—to St. Peter Robinson's, and spread the silks of the earth before her feet, and see the awakening delight in her eyes and the glow on her cheek; to buy a pony for the "kids" and a diamond brooch for the kind, middle-aged matron who befriended you years since in time of financial need; to get a new gun, and inquire about the price of a deer-stalk in Scotland; whetting the road now and then with a sip of Moet—but only one sip, for your liver's sake—just to brighten up the imagination. And so onwards in a widening circle, as sun-lit fancy led: could Xerxes, could great Pompey, could Cæsar with all his legions, could Lucullus with all his oysters, ever have enjoyed such pleasure as this—just to spend money freely, with a jolly chuckle, in the streets of London? What is Mahomet's Paradise to that?

The exquisite delight of utterly abandoned extravagance, no

counting—anathemas on counting and calculation! If life be not a dream, what is the use of living?

Say what you will, the truth is, we all struggle on in hope of living in a dream some day. This is my dream. Dreadfully, horribly wicked, is it not, in an age that preaches thrift and—twaddle? No joy like waste in London streets; happy waste, imaginative extravagance; to and fro like a butterfly!

Besides, there's no entertainment in the world like the streets of London on a sunny day or a gas-lit night. The shops, the carriages, the people, the odds and ends of life one sees, the drifting to and fro of folk, the "bits" of existence, glimpses into shadowy corners, the dresses, the women; dear me, where shall we get to? At all events, the fact remains that to anyone with an eye the best entertainment in the world is a lounge in London streets. Theatres, concerts, séances, Albert Halls, museums, galleries, are but set and formal shows; a great weariness, for the most part, and who the deuce would care to go and gaze at them again who could lounge in Piccadilly?

It is well worth a ten-pound note any day in May; fifty pounds sometimes at 1 p.m., merely to look on, I mean, it is worth it; but you can see this living show for nothing. Let the grandees go to the opera; for me, the streets.

So I can't throw dirt at Raleigh, who often had a hatful of money, and could and did just what seemed pleasant in his sight. But the money went like water, and in order to get further supplies, the idle, good-for-nothing, lazy dog worked like a prime minister with telegrams, letters, newspapers, and so on, worked like a prime minister—at betting. Horse-racing, in short, was the explanation of the memorandum-book, the load of correspondence, and the telegrams, kept flat with a glass of whiskey as a paper-weight.

While he wrote, and thought, and reckoned up his chances, a loud refrain of snoring arose from the sofa. It was almost as loud as the boom of the fair, but Raleigh had no nerves. His friend Freddie, becoming oppressed with so much labour, had dropped asleep, leaving his whiskey beside him on the sofa, so that the first time he moved over it went on the carpet. With one long leg stretched out, the other knee up, lying on his back, and his mouth wide open to the ceiling, Freddie was very happy.

Raleigh puffed his clay pipe, sipped, and puffed again. Freddie boomed away on the sofa. The family was in London; Raleigh and Freddie got down here in this way: it happened one night there was a row at a superb bar, Haymarket trail. The "chuckers-out" began their coarse horse-play, and in the general melée Raleigh distinguished himself. Rolled about by the crowd, he chanced to find himself for a moment in a favourable position, and punished one of these gigantic brutes pretty severely.

Though stout and short of breath, Raleigh was strong in the arm, he was "up," and he hit hard. The fellow's face was a "picture," coloured in cardinal. Such an opportunity does not occur twice in a lifetime; Raleigh's genius seized the opportunity, and he became great. Actium was a trifle to it.

There were mighty men before Agamemnon, and there are mighty men who do not figure in the papers.

Raleigh became at once an anaxandron—a King of Men. The history of his feat spread in ten minutes from one end of midnight London to the other: from the policeman in Waterloo Place to—everywhere. Never was such a stir; the fall of Sebastopol—dear me! I can remember it, look at the flight of time—was nothing to it. They would have chaired him, fêted him, got a band to play him about the place, literally crowned him with laurel. Ave, Cæsar! Evœ! Bacchus! But they could not find him.

Raleigh was off with Freddie, who had been in at the death, and was well "blooded." Hansom to Paddington in the small hours; creep, creep, creep, through the raw morning mist, puff, whistle, broad gauge, and they had vanished.

Raleigh was a man of his age; he lost not a moment; having got the glory, the next thing was to elude the responsibility; and, in short, he slipped out of sight till the hue-and-cry was over, and the excitement of the campaign had subsided.

In case anyone should suppose I approve of midnight battle, I may as well label the account at once: "This is a goak."

I do not approve of brawls at the bar, but I have set myself the task to describe a bit of human life exactly as it really is, and I can assure you as a honest fact that Raleigh by that lucky knock became a very great man indeed among people as they really are. People as they really are, are not all Greek scholars.

As I don't wish you to look down upon poor Raleigh too much because he smoked a cutty, and hit a fellow twice as big as himself, and lent his money, and made bets, and drank whiskey, and was altogether wicked, I may as well tell you something in his favour: He was a hero to his valet.

"No man is a hero to his valet," says the proverb, not even Napoleon, Disraeli, or Solomon.

But Raleigh was a hero to his valet.

He was not only a hero to Nobbs the valet; he had perfectly fascinated him. The instant he was off duty Nobbs began to be a Raleigh to himself. He put on a coat cut in the Raleigh careless style; in fact, he dressed himself Raleigh all over. His private hat was exactly like Raleigh's; so was his necktie, the same colour, shape, and bought at the same shop; so were his boots. He kept a sovereign loose in his waistcoat pocket, because that was where Raleigh carried his handy gold. He smoked a cutty-pipe, and drank endless whiskies—just like Raleigh, "the very ticket"—he had his betting-book, and his telegrams, and his money on "hosses," and his sporting paper, and his fine photographs of fine women. He swore in Raleigh's very words, and used to spit like him; Raleigh, if ever he chanced to expectorate, had an odd way of twisting up the corner of his mouth, so did Nobbs. In town Nobbs went to the very same bars (always, of course, discreetly and out of sight), the very same theatres; a most perfect Raleigh to the tiniest detail. Why, Raleigh very rarely wound up his watch—careless Raleigh; accordingly, Nobbs' watch was seldom going. "And you just look here," said Nobbs to a great and confidential friend, after they had done endless whiskies, and smoked handfuls of Raleigh's tobacco, "you look here, if I was he, and had lots of chink, and soft old parties to get money out of as easy as filling yer pipe, by Jove! wouldn't I cut a swell! I'd do it, I would. I'd make that Whitechapel of his spin along, I rather guess I would. I'd liquor up. Wouldn't I put a thou on the Middle Park Plate? Ah! wouldn't I, Tommy, my boy! Just wouldn't I have heaps of wimmen; some in the trap, and some indoors, and some to go to the theatre with—respectable gals, I mean—crowds of 'em would come if Raleigh was to hold up his finger. Guess I'd fill this old shop (the Pamment mansion) choke full of wimmen! If I was only he! Shouldn't I like to fetch one of them waiter chaps a swop on the nose, like he did! Oh, my! Oh, Tommy!" And Nobbs very nearly wept at the happy vision of being "he."

Why, Raleigh was not only a Hero, he was a Demi-god to his valet! Not only Nobbs, but the footmen, and the grooms, and the whole race of servants everywhere who had caught a glimpse of Raleigh looked upon him as the Ideal Man. So did the whole race of "cads" in the bars and at the races, and all over town and country, all of that sort who knew anything of Raleigh sighed to be like "he."

The fellow who said that "No man is a hero to his valet" seemed to suppose that the world worships good and divine qualities only. Nothing of the sort; it is not the heroic, it is the low and coarse and blackguard part the mass of people regard with such deep admiration.

If only Nobbs could have been "he," no doubt whatever he would have "done it" very big indeed. But he would have left out of his copy that part of Raleigh's nature which, in spite of the whiskey and the cutty, and the rest of it, made him still a perfect gentleman at heart. Nobbs didn't want to be a perfect gentleman.

CHAPTER XVII

GLANCING up from his betting-book, Raleigh caught sight of someone on the lawn, and went to the window to see who it was.

It was then that Grandfather Iden raised his great grey hat, and brought it with so lowly a sweep down to the very ground before this demi-god of his.

"Hullo! Fred, I say! Come, quick!" dragging him off the sofa. "Here's the Behemoth."

"The Behemoth—the Deluge!" said Fred, incoherently, still half asleep.

"Before that," said Raleigh. "I told you I'd show him to you some day. That's the Behemoth."

Some grand folk keep a hump-backed cow, or white wild cattle, or strange creatures of that sort, in their parks as curiosities. The particular preserve of the Pamments was Grandfather Iden—antediluvian Iden—in short, the Behemoth.

It is not everybody who has got a Behemoth on show.

"There's a girl with him," said Fred.

"Have her in," said Raleigh. "Wake us up," ringing the bell. And he ordered the butler to fetch old Iden in.

How thoroughly in character with Human Life it was that a man like Grandfather Iden—aged, experienced, clever, learned, a man of wise old books, should lower his ancient head, and do homage to Raleigh Pamment!

"Wherefore come ye not to court?
Skelton swears 'tis glorious sport.
Chattering fools and wise men listening."

Accordingly the butler went out bare-headed—his head was as bare as Mont Blanc—and, with many a gracious smile, conveyed his master's wishes. The Behemoth, mopping and mowing, wiping his slobbery old mouth in the excess of his glorification, takes Amaryllis by the arm, and proceeds to draw her towards the mansion.

"But, grandpa—grandpa—really I'd rather not go. Please, don't make me go. No—no—I can't," she cried, in a terror of disgust. She would not willingly have set foot on the Pamment threshold, no, not for a crown of gold, as the old song says unctuously.

"Don't be afraid," said Iden. "Nothing to be afraid of"—mistaking her hesitation for awe.

"Afraid!" repeated Amaryllis, in utter bewilderment. "Afraid! I don't want to go."

"There's nothing to be afraid of, I'm sure," said the butler in his most insidious tones. "Mr. Pamment so very particularly wished to see you."

"Come—come," said old Iden, "don't be silly," as she still hung back. "It's a splendid place inside—there, lean on me, don't be afraid," and so the grandfather pulling her one side, and the butler very, very gently pressing her forward the other, they persuaded, or rather they moved Amaryllis onward.

She glanced back, her heart beat quick, she had half a mind to break loose—easy enough to over-turn the two old fogies—but—how soon "but" comes, "but" came to Amaryllis at sixteen. She remembered her father. She remembered her mother's worn-out boots. By yielding yet a little further she could perhaps contrive to keep her grandfather in good humour and open the way to a reconciliation.

So the revolutionary Amaryllis, the red-hot republican blood seething like molten metal in her veins, stepped across the hated threshold of the ancient and mediæval Pamments.

But we have all heard about taking the horse to water and finding that he would not drink. If you cannot even make a horse, do you think you are likely to make a woman do anything?

Amaryllis walked beside her grandfather quietly enough now, but she would not see or hear; he pointed out to her the old armour, the marble, the old oak; he mumbled on of the staircase where John Pamment, temp. Hen. VII., was seized for high treason; she kept her glance steadfastly on the ground.

Iden construed it to be veneration, and was yet more highly pleased.

Raleigh had taste enough to receive them in another room, not the whiskey-room; he met old Iden literally with open arms, taking both the old gentleman's hands in his he shook them till Iden tottered, and tears came into his eyes.

Amaryllis scarcely touched his fingers, and would not raise her glance.

"Raw," thought Freddie, who being tall looked over Raleigh's shoulder. "Very raw piece."

To some young gentlemen a girl is a "piece."

"My granddaughter," said Iden, getting his voice.

"Ah, yes; like to see the galleries—fond of pictures——"

Amaryllis was silent.

"Answer," said Grandfather Iden graciously, as much as to say, "you may."

"No," said Amaryllis.

"Hum—let's see—books—library—carvings. Come, Mr. Iden, you know the place better than I do, you're an antiquarian and a scholar—I've forgotten my Greek. What would you like to show her?"

"She is fond of pictures," said Iden, greatly flattered that he should be thought to know the house better than the heir. "She is fond of pictures; she's shy."

Amaryllis' face became a dark red. The rushing blood seemed to stifle her. She could have cried out aloud; her pride only checked her utterance.

Raleigh, not noticing the deep colour in her face, led on upstairs, down the corridors, and into the first saloon. There he paused and old Iden took the lead, going straight to a fine specimen of an old Master.

Holding his great grey hat (which he would not give up to the butler) at arm's-length and pointing, the old man began to show Amaryllis the beauties of the picture.

"A grand thing—look," said he.

"I can't see," said Amaryllis, forced to reply.

"Not see!" said Iden, in a doubtful tone.

"Not a good light, perhaps," said Raleigh. "Come this side."

She did not move.

"Go that side," said Iden.

No movement.

"Go that side," he repeated, sharply.

At last she moved over by Raleigh and stood there, gazing down still.

"Look up," said Iden. She looked up hastily—above the canvas, and then again at the floor.

Iden's dim old eyes rested a moment on the pair as they stood together; Amaryllis gazing downwards, Raleigh gazing at her. Thoughts of a possible alliance, perhaps, passed through Iden's mind; only consider, intermarriage between the Pamments and the Idens! Much more improbable things have happened; even without the marriage license the connection would be an immense honour.

Grandfather Iden, aged ninety years, would most certainly have sacrificed the girl of sixteen, his own flesh and blood, joyously and intentionally to his worship of the aristocrat.

If she could not have been the wife he would have forced her to be the mistress.

There is no one so cruel—so utterly inhuman—as an old man, to whom feeling, heart, hope have long been dead words.

"Now you can see," he said, softly and kindly. "Is it not noble?"

"It looks smoky," said Amaryllis, lifting her large, dark eyes at last and looking her grandfather in the face.

"Smoky!" he ejaculated, dropping his great white hat, his sunken cheeks flushing. It was not so much the remark as the tone of contemptuous rebellion.

"Smoky," he repeated.

"Smoky and—dingy," said Amaryllis. She had felt without actually seeing that Raleigh's gaze had been fixed upon her the whole time since they had entered, that emphatic look which so pleases or so offends a woman.

Now there was nothing in Raleigh's manner to give offence— on the contrary he had been singularly pleasant, respectfully pleasant—but she remembered the fellow staring at her from the window at the "Lamb" and it biased her against him. She wished to treat him, and his pictures, and his place altogether with marked contempt.

"I do not care for these pictures," she said. "I will leave now, if you please," and she moved towards the door.

"Stop!" cried Iden, stretching out his hands and tottering after her. "Stop! I order you to stop! you rude girl!"

He could not catch her, she had left the gallery—he slipped in his haste on the polished floor. Fred caught him by the arm or he would have fallen, and at the same time presented him with his great white hat.

"Ungrateful!" he shrieked, and then choked and slobbered and mumbled, and I verily believe had it not been for his veneration of the place he would have spat upon the floor.

Raleigh had rushed after Amaryllis, and overtook her at the staircase.

"Pardon me, Miss Iden," he said, as she hastily descended. "Really I should have liked you to have seen the house—will you sit down a moment? Forgive me if I said or did——. No, do stay— please—" as she made straight for the hall. "I am so sorry—really sorry—unintentional"—in fact he had done nothing, and yet he was penitent. But she would not listen, she hurried on along the path, she began to run, or nearly, as he kept up with her, still begging her to pause; Amaryllis ran at last outright. "At least let me see you through the fair—rough people. Let me open the door——"

The iron-studded door in the wall shut with a spring lock, and for a moment she could not unfasten it; she tore at it and grazed her hand, the blood started.

"Good Heavens!" cried Raleigh, now thoroughly upset. "Let

me bind it up," taking out his handkerchief. "I would not have had this happen for money"—short for any amount of money. "Let me—"

"Do please leave me," cried Amaryllis, panting, not with the run, which was nothing to her, but pent-up indignation, and still trying to open the lock.

Raleigh pressed the lock and the door swung open—he could easily have detained her there, but he did not. "One moment, pray— Miss Iden." She was gone down the passage between the Abbey church and the wall; he followed, she darted out into the crowd of the fair.

CHAPTER XVIII

WHEN he stopped and turned, angry beyond measure, vexation biting deep lines like aquafortis on his broad, good-natured face.

"That I should have been such a fool—an infernal blockheaded fool—" shutting the iron-studded door with a kick and a clang— "muddle-headed fool—I'll never touch a drop of whiskey again—and that jackass, Fred—why, she's—" a lady, he would have said, but did not dare admit to himself now that he had thought to ask her in to "wake us up." "But what did I do? Can't think what annoyed her. Must have been something between her and that tedious old Iden. Quite sure I didn't do or say——" but still he could not quiet his conscience, for if he had not by deed or word, he knew he had in thought.

He had sent for her as he might have done for any of the vulgar wenches in the fair to amuse an idle hour, and he was ashamed of himself.

In truth, Raleigh had never seen a woman like Amaryllis Iden. Her features were not beautiful, as general ideas go, nor had her form the grace of full increase; indeed words, and even a portrait by a master-hand, would have failed to carry the impression her nature had made upon him.

It is not the particular cast of features that makes a man great, and gives him a pre-eminence among his fellows. It is the character—the mind.

A great genius commands attention at once by his presence, and so a woman may equally impress by the power of her nature. Her moral strength asserts itself in subtle ways.

I don't say for certain that it was her character that impressed Raleigh—it might have been nothing of the sort, it might have been because it was so, a woman's reason, and therefore appropriate. These things do not happen by "why and because."

Some may say it is quite out of place to suppose a whiskey-sipping, cutty-pipe smoking, horse-racing, bar-frequenting fellow like Raleigh could by any possible means fall in love at first sight. But whiskey, cutty, horse, and bar were not the real man, any more than your hat is your head, they were mere outside chaff, he had a sound heart all the same, a great deal sounder and better, and infinitely more generous than some very respectable folk who are regularly seen in their pews, and grind down their clerks and dependents to the edge of starvation.

Raleigh was capable of a good deal of heart, such as the pew-haunting Pharisee knows not of. Perhaps he was not in love: at all events he was highly excited.

Fred had contrived to keep old Iden from following Amaryllis by representing that Raleigh would be sure to bring her back. The butler, who was very well acquainted with old Iden, hastily whipped out a bottle of champagne and handed him a brimming glass. The old gentleman, still mouthing and bubbling over with rage, spluttered and drank, and spluttered again, and refusing a second, would go, and so met Raleigh in the hall.

Raleigh tried on his part to soothe the old man, and on his part the old man tried at one and the same moment to apologize for his granddaughter and to abuse her for her misconduct. Consequently neither of them heard or understood the other.

But no sooner was Iden gone than Raleigh, remembering the rough crowd in the fair, despatched the butler after him to see him safe home. It was now growing dusky as the evening came on.

Without more ado, this young gentleman then set to and swore at Fred for half an hour straight ahead. Fred at first simply stared and wondered what on earth had turned his brain; next, being equally hot-tempered, he swore in reply; then there followed some sharp recriminations (for each knew too much of the other's goings on not to have plenty of material), and finally they sparred. Two or three cuffs cooled their ardour, having nothing to quarrel about; sulks ensued; Raleigh buried himself in the papers; Fred lit a cigar and walked out into the fair. Thus there was tribulation in the great house of the Pamments.

Grandfather Iden permitted the butler to steer him through

the crowd quietly enough, because it flattered him to be thus taken care of before the world by a Pamment servitor. When they parted at the doorstep he slipped half-a-sovereign in the butler's hand—he could not offer less than gold to a Pamments' man—but once inside, his demeanour changed. He pushed away his housekeeper, went into his especial sitting-room, bolted the door, spread his hands and knees over the fire, and poked the coals, grunted, poked, and stirred till smoke and smuts filled the stuffy little place.

By-and-by there was a banging of drawers—the drawers in the bureau and the bookcases were opened and shut sharply—writing-paper was flung on the table, and he sat down to write a letter with a scratchy quill pen. The letter written was ordered to post immediately, and the poking, and stirring, and grunting recommenced. Thus there was tribulation in the house of the head of the Idens.

Amaryllis meantime had got through the town by keeping between the booths and the houses. Just as she left the last street Ned Marks rode up—he had been on the watch, thinking to talk with her as she walked home, but just as he drew rein to go slow and so speak, a heathen pig from the market rushed between his horse's legs and spoiled the game by throwing him headlong.

She did not see, or at least did not notice, but hastening on, entered the fields. In coming to town that morning she had seen everything; now, returning in her anger and annoyance, she took no heed of anything; she was so absorbed that when a man—one of those she met going to the fair for the evening—turned back and followed her some way, she did not observe him. Finding that she walked steadily on, the fellow soon ceased to pursue.

The gloom had settled when she reached home, and the candles were lit. She gave her father the sovereign, and was leaving the room, hoping to escape questioning, when Mrs. Iden asked who had the prize-guinea.

"I did," said Amaryllis, very quietly and reluctantly.

"Where is it? Why didn't you say so? Let me see," said Mrs. Iden.

"I—I—I lost it," said Amaryllis.

"You lost it! Lost a guinea! A spade-guinea!"

"What!" said Iden in his sternest tones. "Show it immediately."

"I can't; I lost it."

"Lost it!"

And they poured upon her a cross-fire of anger: a careless, wasteful hussy, an idle wretch; what did she do for her living that she could throw away spade-guineas? what would her grandfather

76

say? how did she suppose they were to keep her, and she not earn the value of a bonnet-string? time she was apprenticed to a dressmaker; the quantity she ate, and never could touch any fat—dear me, so fine—bacon was not good enough for her—she could throw away spade-guineas.

Poor Amaryllis stood by the half-open door, her hat in her hand, her bosom heaving, her lips apart and pouting, not with indignation but sheer misery; her head drooped, her form seemed to lose its firmness and sink till she stooped; she could not face them as she would have done others, because you see she loved them, and she had done her best that day till too sorely tried.

The storm raged on; finally Iden growled "Better get out of sight." Then she went to her bedroom, and sat on the bed; presently she lay down, and sobbed silently on the pillow, after which she fell asleep, quite worn out, dark circles under her eyes. In the silence of the house, the tom-tom and blare of brazen instruments blown at the fair two miles away was audible.

CHAPTER XIX

So there was tribulation in three houses. Next morning she scarcely dared come in to breakfast, and opened the door timidly, expecting heavy looks, and to be snapped up if she spoke. Instead of which, on taking her place, Iden carefully cut for her the most delicate slice of ham he could find, and removed the superfluous fat before putting it on her plate. Mrs. Iden had a special jug of cream ready for her—Amaryllis was fond of cream—and enriched the tea with it generously.

"And what did you see at the fair?" asked Iden in his kindest voice, lifting up his saucer—from which he always drank—by putting his thumb under it instead of over, so that his thick little finger projected. He always sipped his tea in this way.

"You had plenty of fun, didn't you?" said Mrs. Iden, still more kindly.

"I—I don't know; I did not see much of the fair," said Amaryllis, at a loss to understand the change of manner.

Iden smiled at his wife and nodded; Mrs. Iden picked up a letter from the tea-tray and gave it to her daughter:

"Read."

Amaryllis read—it was from Grandfather Iden, furiously upbraiding Iden for neglecting his daughter's education; she had no reverence, no manners—an undutiful, vulgar girl; she had better not show her face in his house again till she had been taught to know her position; her conduct was not fit for the kitchen; she had not the slightest idea how to behave herself in the presence of persons of quality.

She put it down before she had finished the tirade of abuse; she did not look up, her face was scarlet.

Iden laughed.

"Horrid old wretch! Served him right!" said Mrs. Iden. "So glad you vexed him, dear!"

Amaryllis last night a wretch was this morning a heroine. The grandfather's letter had done this.

Iden never complained—never mentioned his father—but of course in his heart he bitterly felt the harsh neglect shown towards him and his wife and their child. He was a man who said the less the more he was moved; he gossiped freely with the men at the stile, or even with a hamlet old woman. Not a word ever dropped from him of his own difficulties—he kept his mind to himself. His wife knew nothing of his intentions—he was over-secretive, especially about money matters, in which he affected the most profound mystery, as if everyone in Coombe was not perfectly aware they could hardly get a pound of sugar on credit.

All the more bitterly he resented the manner in which Grandfather Iden treated him, giving away half-crowns, crown-pieces, shillings, and fourpenny bits to anyone who would flatter his peculiarities, leaving his own descendants to struggle daily with debt and insult.

Iden was in reality a very proud man, and the insults of his petty creditors fretted him.

He would have been glad if Amaryllis had become her grandfather's favourite; as the grandfather had thrown savage words at the girl, so much the more was added to the score against the grandfather.

Mrs. Iden hated the grandfather with every drop of Flamma blood in her veins—hated him above all for his pseudo-Flamma relationship, for old Iden had in his youth been connected with the Flammas in business—hated him for his veneration of the aristocratic and mediæval Pamments.

She was always impressing upon Amaryllis the necessity of

78

cultivating her grandfather's goodwill, and always abusing him—contradicting herself in the most natural manner.

This letter had given them such delight, because it showed how deeply Amaryllis had annoyed the old gentleman. Had he been whipped he could hardly have yelled more; he screamed through his scratchy quill. Suppose they did lose his money, he had had one good upset, that was something.

They were eager to hear all about it. Amaryllis was at first very shy to tell, knowing that her father was a thick Tory and an upholder of the Pamments, and fearing his displeasure. But for various reasons both father and mother grew warmer in delight at every fresh incident of her story.

Mrs. Flamma Iden—revolutionary Flamma—detested the Pamments enthusiastically, on principle first, and next, because the grandfather paid them such court.

Iden was indeed an extra thick Tory, quite opaque, and had voted in the Pamment interest these thirty years, yet he had his secret reasons for disliking them personally.

Both Mr. and Mrs. Iden agreed in their scorn of the grandfather's pottering about the grounds and in and out the conservatories, as if that was the highest honour on earth. Yet Mrs. Iden used often to accuse her husband of a desire to do the very same thing: "You're just as stupid," she would say; "you'd think it wonderful to have a private key—you're every bit as silly really, only you haven't got the chance."

However, from a variety of causes they agreed in looking on Amaryllis' disgrace as a high triumph and glory.

So she was petted all the morning by both parties—a rare thing—and in the afternoon Iden gave her the sovereign she had brought home, to buy her some new boots, and to spend the rest as she chose on herself.

Away went Amaryllis to the town, happy and yet not without regret that she had increased the disagreement between her father and grandfather. She met the vans and gipsies slowly leaving the site of the fair, the children running along with bare brown feet. She went under the archæologically interesting gateway, and knocked at the door of Tiras Wise, shoemaker, "established 200 years."

Tiras Wise of the present generation was thin and nervous, weary of the centuries, worn out, and miserable-looking. Amaryllis, strong in the possession of a golden sovereign, attacked him sharply for his perfidious promises; her boots promised at Christmas were not mended yet.

Tiras, twiddling a lady's boot in one hand, and his foot measure in the other, very humbly and deprecatingly excused himself; there had been so much trouble with the workmen, some were so tipsy, and some would not work; they were always demanding higher wages, and just as he had a job in hand going off and leaving it half finished—shoemaker's tricks these. Sometimes, indeed, he could not get a workman, and then there was the competition of the ready-made boot from Northampton; really, it was most trying—it really was.

"Well, and when am I going to have the boots?" said Amaryllis, amused at the poor fellow's distress. "When are they going to be finished?"

"You see, Miss Iden," said the shoemaker's mother, coming to help her son, "the fact is, he's just worried out of his life with his men—and really—"

"You don't seem to get on very well with your shoemaking, Mr. Wise," said the customer, smiling.

"The fact is," said poor Wise, in his most melancholy manner, with a deep sigh, "the fact is, the men don't know their work as they used to, they spoil the leather and cut it wrong, and leave jobs half done, and they're always drinking; the leather isn't so good as it used to be; the fact is," with a still deeper sigh, "we can't make a boot."

At which Amaryllis laughed outright, to think that people should have been in business two hundred years as shoemakers, and yet could not make a boot!

Her experience of life as yet was short, and she saw things in their first aspect; it is not till much later we observe that the longer people do one thing, the worse they do it, till in the end they cannot do it at all.

She presently selected a pair for herself, 9s., and another pair for her mother, 10s. 6d., leaving sixpence over; add sixpence discount for ready-money, and she was still rich with a shilling. Carrying the parcel, she went up the street and passed old Iden's door on elate instep, happy that she had not got to cross his threshold that day, happy to think she had the boots for her mother. Looking in at two or three dingy little shops, she fixed at last on one, and bought half-a-dozen of the very finest mild bloaters, of which Mrs. Iden was so fond. This finished the savings, and she turned quickly for home. The bloaters being merely bound round with one thin sheet of newspaper, soon imparted their odour to her hand.

A lady whose hand smells of bloaters is not, I hope, too ideal; I hope you will see now that I am not imaginative, or given to the heroinesque. Amaryllis, I can tell you, was quite absorbed in the bloaters and the boots; a very sweet, true, and loving hand it was, in spite of the bloaters—one to kiss fervently.

They soon had the bloaters on over a clear fire of wood-coals, and while they cooked the mother tried her new boots, naturally not a little pleased with the thoughtful present. The Flamma blood surged with gratitude; she would have given her girl the world at that moment. That she should have remembered her mother showed such a good disposition; there was no one like Amaryllis.

"Pah!" said Iden, just then entering, "pah!" with a gasp; and holding his handkerchief to his nose, he rushed out faster than he came in, for the smell of bloaters was the pestilence to him.

They only laughed all the merrier over their supper.

CHAPTER XX

RIGHT at the top of the house there was a large, unfurnished room, which Amaryllis had taken as her own long since. It was her study, her thinking-room, her private chapel and praying-room, her one place of solitude, silence, and retirement.

The days had gone on, and it was near the end of April. Coming up the dark stairs one morning, she found them still darker, because she had just left the sunshine. They were built very narrow, as usual in old country-houses, and the landing shut off with a door, so that when you were in them you seemed to be in a box. There was no carpet—bare boards; old-fashioned folk did not carpet their stairs; no handrail; the edges of the steps worm-eaten and ragged, little bits apt to break off under sudden pressure, so that the board looked as if it had been nibbled by mice.

Shutting the landing door behind her, Amaryllis was in perfect darkness, but her feet knew the well-remembered way, and she came quickly to the top.

There were two great rooms running the whole length of the house: the first was a lumber-room, the second her own especial cell. Cell-like it was, in its monastic or conventual bareness. It was vague with bareness: a huge, square room, gaunt as a barn, the walls and ceiling whitewashed, the floor plain boards. Yonder, near the one small window, stood a table and tall-backed oaken chair, afar off, as it were, from the doorway—a journey to them across the creaking floor. On one side an old four-post bedstead of dark oak,

81

much damaged, was placed by the wall; the sacking hung down in a loop, torn and decayed—a bedstead on which no one had slept these hundred years past. By the table there was, too, an ancient carved linen-press of black oak, Amaryllis' bookcase.

These bits of rude furniture were lost in the vastness of space, as much as if you had thrown your hat into the sky.

Amaryllis went straight to the window and knelt down. She brought a handful of violets, fresh-gathered, to place in the glass which she kept there for her flowers. The window was cut in the thick wall, and formed a niche, where she always had a tumbler ready—a common glass tumbler, she could not afford a vase.

They were the white wild violets, the sweetest of all, gathered while the nightingale was singing his morning song in the April sunshine—a song the world never listens to, more delicious than his evening notes, for the sunlight helps him, and the blue of the heavens, the green leaf, and the soft wind—all the soul of spring.

White wild violets, a dewdrop as it were of flower, tender and delicate, growing under the great hawthorn hedge, by the mosses and among the dry, brown leaves of last year, easily overlooked unless you know exactly where to go for them. She had a bunch for her neck, and a large bunch for her niche. They would have sunk and fallen into the glass, but she hung them by their chins over the edge of the tumbler, with their stalks in the water. Then she sat down in the old chair at the table, and rested her head on her hand.

Except where she did this every day, and so brushed it, a thin layer of dust had covered the surface (there was no cloth) and had collected on her portfolio, thrust aside and neglected. Dust on the indiarubber, dust on the cake of Indian ink, dust invisible on the smooth surface of the pencils, dust in the little box of vine charcoal.

The hoarse baying of the hungry wolves around the house had shaken the pencil from her fingers—Siberian wolves they were, racing over the arid deserts of debt, large and sharp-toothed, ever increasing in number and ferocity, ready to tear the very door down. There are no wolves like those debt sends against a house.

Every knock at the door, every strange footstep up the approach, every letter that came, was like the gnawing and gnashing of savage teeth.

Iden could plant the potatoes and gossip at the stile, and put the letters unopened on the mantelshelf—a pile of bills over his head where he slept calmly after dinner. Iden could plant potatoes, and cut trusses of hay, and go through his work to appearance unmoved.

Amaryllis could not draw—she could not do it; her imagination refused to see the idea; the more she concentrated her mind, the louder she heard the ceaseless grinding and gnashing of teeth.

Potatoes can be planted and nails can be hammered, bill-hooks can be wielded and faggots chopped, no matter what the inward care. The ploughman is deeply in debt, poor fellow, but he can, and does, follow the plough, and finds, perhaps, some solace in the dull monotony of his labour. Clods cannot feel. A sensitive mind and vivid imagination—a delicately-balanced organization, that almost lives on its ideas as veritable food—cannot do like this. The poet, the artist, the author, the thinker, cannot follow their plough; their work depends on a serene mind.

But experience proves that they do do their work under such circumstances. They do; how greatly then they must be tortured, or for what a length of time they must have suffered to become benumbed.

Amaryllis was young, and all her feelings unchecked of Time. She could not sketch—that was a thing of useless paper and pencil; what was wanted was money. She could not read, that was not real; what was wanted was solid coin.

So the portfolio was thrust aside, neglected and covered with dust, but she came every day to her flowers in the window-niche.

She had drawn up there in the bitter cold of February and March, without a fire, disdainful of ease in the fulness of her generous hope. Her warm young blood cared nothing for the cold, if only by enduring it she could assist those whom she loved.

There were artists in the Flamma family in London who made what seemed to her large incomes, yet whose names had never been seen in a newspaper criticism, and who had never even sent a work to the Academy—never even tried to enter. Their work was not of an ambitious order, but it was well paid.

Amaryllis did not for a moment anticipate success as an artist, nor think to take the world by storm with her talent. Her one only hope was to get a few pounds now and then—she would have sold twenty sketches for ten shillings—to save her father from insult, and to give her mother the mere necessities of dress she needed.

No thought of possible triumph, nor was she sustained by an overmastering love of art; she was inspired by her heart, not her genius.

Had circumstances been different she would not have earnestly practised drawing; naturally she was a passive rather than an active artist.

She loved beauty for its own sake—she loved the sunlight, the grass and trees, the gleaming water, the colours of the fields and of the sky. To listen to the running water was to her a dear delight, to the wind in the high firs, or caught in the wide-stretching arms of the oak; she rested among these things, they were to her mind as sleep to the body. The few good pictures she had seen pleased her, but did not rouse the emotion the sunlight caused; artificial music was enjoyable, but not like the running stream. It said nothing—the stream was full of thought.

No eager desire to paint like that or play like that was awakened by pictures or music; Amaryllis was a passive and not an active artist by nature. And I think that is the better part; at least, I know it is a thousand times more pleasure to me to see a beautiful thing than to write about it. Could I choose I would go on seeing beautiful things, and not writing.

Amaryllis had no ambition whatever for name or fame; to be silent in the sunshine was enough for her. By chance she had inherited the Flamma talent—she drew at once without effort or consideration; it was not so much to her as it is to me to write a letter.

The thought to make use of her power did not occur to her until the preceding Christmas. Roast beef and plum pudding were a bitter mockery at Coombe Oaks—a sham and cold delusion, cold as snow. A "merry Christmas"—holly berries, mistletoe—and behind these—debt. Behind the glowing fire, written in the flames—debt; in the sound of the distant chimes—debt. Now be merry over the plum-pudding while the wolves gnash their teeth, wolves that the strongest bars cannot keep out.

Immediately the sacred day was past they fell in all their fury upon Iden. Pay me that thou owest! The one only saying in the Gospel thoroughly engrained in the hearts of men. Pay me that thou owest! This is the message from the manger at Bethlehem of our modern Christmas.

CHAPTER XXI

SO Amaryllis went up into the gaunt, cold room at the top of the house, and bent herself seriously to drawing. There was no fireplace, and if there had been they could not have allowed her coals; coals were dear. It was quite an event when the horse and cart went to the wharf for coal. There was plenty of wood for the hearth—wood grew on the farm—but coal was money.

The March winds howled round the corner of the old thatched house, and now and again tremendous rains blew up against the little western window near which she had placed her table. Through the silent cold of January, the moist cold of February, the east winds and hurricane rains of March, Amaryllis worked on in her garret, heedless of nipped fingers and chilled feet.

Sometimes she looked out of the window and watched Iden digging in the garden underneath, planting his potatoes, pruning his trees and shrubs, or farther away, yonder in the meadow, clearing out the furrows that the water might flow better—"trenching," as he called it.

The harder it rained the harder he worked at this in the open, with a sack about his shoulders like a cloak; the labourers were under shelter, the master was out in the wet, hoping by guiding the water to the grass to get a larger crop of hay in June.

Bowed under his sack, with his rotten old hat, he looked a woful figure as the heavy shower beat on his back. But to Amaryllis he was always her father.

Sometimes she went into the next room—the lumber-room—only lighted by a window on a level with the floor, a window which had no glass, but only a wire network. Sitting on the floor there, she could see him at the stile across the road, his hands behind his back, gossiping now with another farmer or two, now with a labourer, now with an old woman carrying home a yoke of water from the brook.

The gossiping hurt Amaryllis even more than the work in the cold rain; it seemed so incongruous, so out of character, so unlike the real Iden as she knew him.

That he, with his great, broad and noble forehead, and his profile like Shakespeare, should stand there talk, talk, talking on the smallest hamlet topics with old women, and labourers, and thickheaded farmers, was to her a bewilderment and annoyance.

She could not understand it, and she resented it. The real Iden she knew was the man of thought and old English taste, who had told her so much by the fireside of that very Shakespeare whom in features he resembled, and of the poets from Elizabethan days downwards. His knowledge seemed to be endless; there was no great author he had not read, no subject upon which he could not at least tell her where to obtain information. Yet she knew he had never had what is now called an education. How clever he must be to know all these things! You see she did not know how wonderful is the gift of observation, which Iden possessed to a degree that was itself genius. Nothing escaped him; therefore his store was great.

No other garden was planted as Iden's garden was, in the best of old English taste, with old English flowers and plants, herbs and trees. In summer time it was a glory to see: a place for a poet, a spot for a painter, loved and resorted to by every bird of the air. Of a bare old farmhouse he had made a beautiful home.

Questions upon questions her opening mind had poured upon him, and to all he had given her an answer that was an explanation. About the earth and about the sea, the rivers, and living things; about the stars and sun, the comet, the wonders of the firmament, of geology and astronomy, of science; there was nothing he did not seem to know.

A man who had crossed the wide ocean as that Ulysses of whom he read to her, and who, like that Ulysses, enjoyed immense physical strength, why was he like this? Why was he so poor? Why did he work in the rain under a sack? Why did he gossip at the stile with the small-brained hamlet idlers?

It puzzled her and hurt her at the same time.

I cannot explain why it was so, any better than Amaryllis; I could give a hundred reasons, and then there would be no explanation—say partly circumstances, partly lack of a profession in which talent would tell, partly an indecision of character—too much thought—and, after all said and done, Fate.

Watching him from the network window, Amaryllis felt her heart drooping, she knew not why, and went back to her drawing unstrung.

She worked very hard, and worked in vain. The sketches all came back to her. Some of them had a torn hole at the corner where they had been carelessly filed, others a thumb-mark, others had been folded wrongly, almost all smelt of tobacco. Neither illustrated papers, periodicals: neither editors nor publishers would have anything to do with them. One or two took more care, and returned the drawings quite clean; one sent a note saying that they promised well.

Poor Amaryllis! They promised well, and she wanted half a sovereign now. If a prophet assured a man that the picture he could not now dispose of would be worth a thousand pounds in fifty years, what consolation would that be to him?

They were all a total failure. So many letters could not be received in that dull place without others in the house seeing what was going on. Once now and then Amaryllis heard a step on the stairs—a shuffling, uncertain step—and her heart began to beat quicker, for she knew it was her mother. Somehow, although she loved her so dearly, she felt that there was not much sympathy between them. She did not understand her mother; the mother did not understand the daughter. Though she was working for her mother's sake, when she heard her mother's step she was ashamed of her work.

Mrs. Iden would come in and shuffle round the room, drawing one foot along the floor in an aggravating way she had, she was not lame, and look out of window, and presently stand behind Amaryllis, and say—

"Ah! you'll never do anything at that. Never do anything. I've seen too much of it. Better come down and warm yourself."

Now this annoyed Amaryllis so much because it seemed so inconsistent. Mrs. Iden blew up her husband for having no enterprise, and then turned round and discouraged her daughter for being enterprising, and this, too, although she was constantly talking about the superiority of the art employments of the Flammas in London to the clodhopper work around her.

Amaryllis could never draw a line till her mother had gone downstairs again, and then the words kept repeating themselves in her ear—"Never do no good at that, never do no good at that."

If we were to stay to analyse deeply, perhaps we should find that Amaryllis was working for a mother of her own imagination, and not for the mother of fact.

Anyone who sits still, writing, drawing, or sewing, feels the cold very much more than those who are moving indoors or out. It was bitterly cold in the gaunt garret, the more so because the wind came unchecked through the wire network of the window in the next room. But for that her generous young heart cared nothing, nor for the still colder wind of failure.

She had no name—no repute, therefore had her drawings been equal to the finest ever produced they would not have been accepted. Until the accident of reputation arises genius is of no avail.

Except an author, or an artist, or a musician, who on earth would attempt to win success by merit? That alone proves how correct the world is in its estimation of them; they must indeed be poor confiding fools. Succeed by merit!

Does the butcher, or the baker, or the ironmonger, or the tallow-chandler rely on personal merit, or purely personal ability for making a business? They rely on a little capital, credit, and much push. The solicitor is first an articled clerk, and works next as a subordinate, his "footing" costs hundreds of pounds, and years of hard labour. The doctor has to "walk the hospitals," and, if he can, he buys a practice. They do not rely on merit.

The three fools—the author, the artist, and the musician—put certain lines on a sheet of paper and expect the world to at once admire their clever ideas.

In the end—but how far is it to the end!—it is true that genius is certain of recognition; the steed by then has grown used to starvation, waiting for the grass to grow. Look about you: Are the prosperous men of business men of merit? are they all clever? are they geniuses? They do not exactly seem to be so.

Nothing so hard as to succeed by merit; no path so full of disappointments; nothing so incredibly impossible.

I would infinitely rather be a tallow-chandler, with a good steady income and no thought, than an author; at the first opportunity I mean to go into the tallow business.

Until the accident of reputation chanced to come to her, Amaryllis might work and work, and hope and sigh, and sit benumbed in her garret, and watch her father, Shakespeare Iden, clearing the furrows in the rain, under his sack.

She had not even a diploma—a diploma, or a certificate, a South Kensington certificate! Fancy, without even a certificate! Misguided child!

What a hideous collection of frumpery they have got there at the Museum, as many acres as Iden's farm, shot over with all the rubbish of the "periods." What a mockery of true art feeling it is! They have not even a single statue in the place. They would shrivel up in horror at a nude model. They teach art—miserable sham, their wretched art culminates in a Christmas card.

Amaryllis had not even been through the South Kensington "grind," and dared to send in original drawings without a certificate. Ignorance, you see, pure clodhopper ignorance.

Failure waited on her labours; the postman brought them all back again.

Yet in her untaught simplicity she had chosen the line which the very highest in the profession would probably have advised her to take. She drew what she knew. The great cart-horse, the old barn up the road, the hollow tree, the dry reeds, the birds, and chanticleer himself—

High was his comb, and coral red withal,
In dents embattled like a castle wall.

Hardly a circumstance of farm life she did not sketch; the fogger with his broad knife cutting hay; the ancient labourer sitting in the wheelbarrow munching his bread-and-cheese, his face a study for Teniers; the team coming home from plough—winter scenes, most of them, because it was winter time. There are those who would give fifty pounds for one of those studies now, crumpled, stained, and torn as they are.

It was a complete failure. Once only she had a gleam of success. Iden picked up the sketch of the dry reeds in the brook, and after looking at it, put it in his "Farmer's Calendar," on the mantelshelf. Amaryllis felt like the young painter whose work is at last hung at the Academy. His opinion was everything to her. He valued her sketch.

Still, that was not money. The cold wind and the chill of failure still entered her garret study. But it was neither of these that at length caused the portfolio to be neglected, she would have worked on and on, hoping against hope, undaunted, despite physical cold and moral check. It was the procession of creditors.

CHAPTER XXII

STEADILY they came over from the town, dunning Iden and distracting Amaryllis in her garret. She heard the heavy footsteps on the path to the door, the thump, thump with the fist (there was neither knocker nor bell, country fashion); more thumping, and then her mother's excuses, so oft repeated, so wearisome, so profitless. "But where is he?" the creditor would persist. "He's up at the Hayes," or "He's gone to Green Hills." "Well, when will he be in?" "Don't know." "But I wants to know when this yer little account is going to be settled." Then a long narration of his wrongs, threats of "doing summat," i.e., summoning, grumble, grumble, and so slow, unwilling steps departing.

Very rude men came down from the villages demanding payment in their rough way—a raw, crude way, brutally insulting to a lady. Iden had long since exhausted his credit in the town; neither butcher, baker, draper, nor anyone else would let them have a shilling's-worth until the shilling had been placed on the counter. He had been forced lately to deal with the little men of the villages— the little butcher who killed once a fortnight; the petty cottagers' baker, and people of that kind. Inferior meat and inferior bread on credit first; coarse language and rudeness afterwards.

One day, the village baker, having got inside the door as Mrs. Iden incautiously opened it, stood there and argued with her, while Amaryllis in the garret put down her trembling pencil to listen.

"Mr. Iden will send it up," said her mother.

"Oh, he'll send it up. When will he send it up?"

"He'll send it up."

"He've a' said that every time, but it beant come yet. You tell un I be come to vetch it."

"Mr. Iden's not in."

"I'll bide till he be in."

"He'll only tell you he'll send it up."

"I'll bide and see un. You've served I shameful. It's nothing but cheating—that's what I calls it—to have things and never pay for um. It's cheating."

Amaryllis tore downstairs, flushed with passion.

"How dare you say such a thing? How dare you insult my mother? Leave the house this moment!"

And with both hands she literally pushed the man, unwilling, but not absolutely resisting, outside, grumbling as he moved that he never insulted nobody, only asked for his money.

A pleasing preparation this for steadiness of hand, calculated to encourage the play of imagination! She could do nothing for hours afterwards.

Just as often Iden was at home, and then it was worse, because it lasted longer. First they talked by the potato-patch almost under the window; then they talked on the path; then they came indoors, and then there were words and grumbling sounds that rose up the staircase. By-and-by they went out again and talked by the gate. At last the creditor departed, and Iden returned indoors to take a glass of ale and sit a moment till the freshness of the annoyance had left his mind. Mrs. Iden then had her turn at him: the old story—why didn't he do something? Amaryllis knew every word as well as if she had been sitting in the room.

How Iden had patience with them Amaryllis could not think; how he could stand, and be argued with, and abused, and threatened, and yet not take the persecutor by the collar and quietly put him in the road, she could not understand.

The truth was he could not help himself; violence would have availed nothing. But to youth it seems as if a few blows are all that is needed to overcome difficulties.

Waller and Co., the tailor—he was his own Co.—walked over regularly once a week; very civil and very persistent, and persistent in vain. How he came to be a creditor was not easy to see, for Iden's coat was a pattern of raggedness, his trousers bare at the knee, and his shabby old hat rotten. But somehow or other there was a five-pound account two years overdue.

Cobb, the butcher at Woolhorton, got off his trap as he went by, at least twice a week, to chivey Iden about his money. Though he would not let them have a mutton chop without payment, whenever there was five shillings to spare for meat it was always taken into his shop, as it was better to have good meat there, if you had to pay cash for meat, than inferior in the village. One day, Amaryllis was waiting for some steak, side by side with a poor woman, waiting for scraps, while Cobb served a grand lady of the town. "Yes, m'm—oh, yes, m'm, certainly, m'm," bows, and scrapes, and washing of hands, all the obsequiousness possible. When the fine lady had gone, "Lar, Mr. Cobb," says the poor woman, "how different you do speak to they to what you do speak to me."

"Oh, yes," replied Cobb, not in the least abashed at having one manner for the poor and another for the rich. "Yes, you see, these ladies they require such a deal of homage."

There was a long bill at Beavan's the grocer's, but that was not much pressed, only a large blue letter about once a month, as Beavan had a very good profit out of them through the butter. Mrs. Iden made excellent butter, which had a reputation, and Beavan took it all at about half-price. If it had been sold to anyone else he would have insisted on payment. So, by parting with the best butter in the county at half-price, they got their tea and sugar without much dunning.

At one time Mrs. Iden became excited and strange in her manner, as if on the point of hysterics, from which Amaryllis divined something serious was approaching, though her mother would say nothing. So it turned out—a bailiff appeared, and took up his quarters in the kitchen. He was very civil and quiet; he sat by the great fire of logs, and offered to help in any way he could. Iden gave him plenty of beer, for one thing. Amaryllis could not go into the kitchen—the dear old place seemed deserted while he was there.

This woke up Iden for the moment. First there was a rummaging about in his old bureau, and a laborious writing of letters, or adding up of figures. Next there was a great personal getting up, a bath, clean linen, shaving, and donning of clothes packed away these years past. In two hours or so Iden came down another man, astonishingly changed, quite a gentleman in every respect, and so handsome in Amaryllis's eyes. Indeed, he was really handsome still, and to her, of course, wonderfully so. If only he would always dress like that!

Iden walked into Woolhorton, but all these preparations had so consumed the time that the bank was shut, the solicitor's offices closed, and there was no means of raising any money that evening. The son passed the father's doorstep—the worn stone step, ground by the generations of customers—he saw the light behind the blind

91

in the little room where Grandfather Iden sat—he might, had he paused and listened, have heard the old man poke the fire, the twenty-thousand-guinea-man—the son passed on, and continued his lonely walk home, the home that held a bailiff.

A makeshift bed had to be made up for the bailiff in the kitchen, and there he remained the night, and was up and had lit the fire for Luce the servant before she was down. The man was certainly very civil, but still there was the shock of it.

Early in the morning Iden went into town again, saw his solicitor, and got a cheque—it was only five-and-twenty or thirty pounds, and the bailiff left.

CHAPTER XXIII

BUT his presence did not die out of the kitchen; they always seemed to feel as if he had been there. The hearth had been stained by a foreign foot, the very poker had been touched by a foreign hand, the rude form at the side by the wall had been occupied by an intruder. Amaryllis had always been so fond of the kitchen—the oldest part of the house, two centuries at least. The wide hearth and immense chimney, up which, when the fire was out, of a winter's night you could see the stars; over which of a windy night you could imagine the witches riding by, borne on the deep howling of the blast; the great beam and the gun slung to it; the heavy oaken table, unpolished, greyish oak; the window in the thick wall, set with yellowish glass; the stone floor, and the walls from which the whitewash peeled in flakes; the rude old place was very dear to her.

Ofttimes they sat there in winter instead of the sitting-room, drawn by its antique homeliness. Mrs. Iden warmed elder wine, and Iden his great cup of Goliath ale, and they roasted chestnuts and apples, while the potatoes—large potatoes—Iden's selected specialities—were baking buried in the ashes. Looking over her shoulder Amaryllis could see the white drift of snow against the window, which was on a level with the ground outside, and so got Iden to tell her stories of the deep snow in the United States, and the thick ice, sawn with saws, or, his fancy roaming on, of the broad and beautiful Hudson River, the river he had so admired in his youth, the river the poets will sing some day; or of his clinging aloft at night in the gale on the banks of Newfoundland, for he had done duty as a sailor. A bold and adventurous man in his youth, why did he gossip at the stile now in his full and prime of manhood?

It would be a long, long tale to tell, and even then only those who have lived in the country and had practical experience could fully comprehend the hopelessness of working a small farm, unless you are of a wholly sordid nature. Iden's nature was not sordid; the very reverse. The beginning, or one of the beginnings, of the quarrel between father and son arose because of this; Grandfather Iden could not forgive his son for making the place beautiful with trees and flowers.

By-and-by the baked potatoes were done, and they had supper on the old and clumsy table, village made and unpolished, except in so far as the stains of cooking operations had varnished it, the same table at which "Jearje," the fogger, sat every morning to eat his breakfast, and every evening to take his supper. What matter? George worked hard and honestly all day, his great arms on the table, spread abroad as he ate, did not injure it.

Great mealy potatoes, cracked open, white as the snow without, floury and smoking; dabs of Mrs. Iden's delicious butter, a little salt and pepper, and there was a dish for a king. The very skins were pleasant—just a taste.

They were not always alone at these kitchen-feasts, sometimes a Flamma from London, sometimes an Iden from over the hill, or others were there. Iden was very hospitable—though most of his guests (family connections) were idle folk, no good to themselves or anybody, still they were made cordially welcome. But others, very high folk, socially speaking (for they had good connections, too, these poor Idens), who had dined at grand London tables, seemed to enjoy themselves most thoroughly on the rude Homeric fare.

For it was genuine, and there was a breadth, an open-handed generosity, a sense of reality about it; something really to eat, though no finger-glasses; Homeric straightforwardness of purpose.

Amaryllis was very fond of the old kitchen; it was the very centre of home. This strange man, this intruding bailiff, trod heavily on her dearest emotions. His shadow remained on the wall though he had gone.

They all felt it, but Amaryllis most of all, and it was weeks before the kitchen seemed to resume its former appearance. Jearje was the one who restored it. He ate so heartily, and spoke so cheerily at breakfast and at supper, it almost made them forget their troubles to see anyone so grateful and pleased with all they did for him. "Thank you, ma'am; dest about a good bit a' bacon, this yer"—

locally the "d" and "j" were often interchangable, dest for jest, or just—"That'll be a' plenty for I, ma'am, doan't want more'n I can yet"—don't want more than I can eat, don't want to be greedy—"Thank you, miss; dest about some ripping good ale, this yer; that it be."

He so thoroughly enjoyed and appreciated the bacon, and the cheese, and the ale; he was like a great, big human dog; you know how we like to see a big dog wag his tail at his food, or put his paws on our knees and laugh, as it were, with his eyes in our face. They petted him, these two women, exactly as if he had been a dog, giving him all the bones, literally and metaphorically, the actual bones of the meat, and any scraps there were, to take home with him (besides his regular meals), and now and then some trifles of clothing for his aged mother. The dog most thoroughly appreciated this treatment; he rolled in it, revelled in it, grew shiny and fat, and glistened with happiness.

Iden petted him, too, to some degree, out of doors, and for much the same reason; his cheery content and willingness, and the absence of the usual selfish niggardliness of effort. George worked willingly and fairly, and, if occasion needed, stayed another hour, or put his shoulder to the wheel of his own accord, and so, having a good employer, and not one minded to take advantage of him, was rewarded in many ways. Iden did not reduce his wages by a shilling or eighteenpence in winter, and gave him wood for firing, half a sack of potatoes, garden produce, or apples, and various other things from time to time.

Living partly indoors, and being of this disposition, Jearje was more like a retainer than a servant, or labourer; a humble member of the family.

It was a sight to see him eat. Amaryllis and Mrs. Iden used often to watch him covertly, just for the amusement it gave them. He went about it as steadily and deliberately as the horses go to plough; no attempt to caracole in the furrow, ready to stand still as long as you like.

Bacon three inches thick with fat: the fat of beef; fat of mutton—anything they could not finish in the sitting-room; the overplus of cabbage or potatoes, savoury or unsavoury; vast slices of bread and cheese; ale, and any number of slop-basins full of tea—the cups were not large enough—and pudding, cold dumpling, hard as wood, no matter what, Jearje ate steadily through it.

A more willing fellow never lived; if Mrs. Iden happened to want anything from the town ever so late, though George had worked hard the long day through from half-past five in the morning, off he would start, without sign of demur, five miles there and back, and come in singing with his burden.

There are such, as George still among the labourer class, in despite of the change of circumstance and sentiment, men who would be as faithful as the faithfullest retainer who ever accompanied a knight of old time to the Crusade. But, observe, for a good man there must be a good master. Proud Iden was a good master, who never forgot that his man was not a piece of mechanism, but flesh and blood and feelings.

Now this great human dog, sprawling his strong arms abroad on the oaken table, warming his heavily-booted feet at the hearth, always with a cheery word and smile, by his constant presence there slowly wore away the impression of the bailiff, and the dear old kitchen came to be itself again.

CHAPTER XXIV

BUT all these shocks and worries and trampling upon her emotions made the pencil tremble in the artist's hand as she worked in the gaunt garret.

One day, as she was returning from Woolhorton, Iden's solicitor, from whom he had borrowed money, overtook her, walked his horse, and began to talk to her in his perky, affected, silly way. Of all the fools in Woolhorton town there was none equal in pure idiotcy to this namby-pamby fellow—it was wonderful how a man of Iden's intelligence could trust his affairs to such a man, the more so as there was at least one good lawyer in the place. This is very characteristic of the farming race; they will work like negroes in the field, and practise the utmost penury to save a little, and be as cautious over a groat as the keenest miser, and then go and trust their most important affairs to some perfect fool of a solicitor. His father, perhaps, or his uncle, or somebody connected with the firm, had a reputation about the era of Waterloo, and upon this tradition they carry their business to a man whom they admit themselves "doan't seem up to much, yon." In the same way, or worse, for there is no tradition even in this case, they will consign a hundred pounds' worth of milk to London on the mere word of a milkman's agent, a man of straw for aught they know, and never so much as go up to town to see if there is such a milk business in existence.

This jackanapes began to talk to Amaryllis about her father. "Now, don't you think, Miss Iden, you could speak to your father about these money matters; you know he's getting into a pound, he really is (the jackanapes pretended to hunt); he'll be pounded. Now, don't you think you could talk to him, and persuade him to be more practical?"

The chattering of this tom-tit upset Amaryllis more than the rudeness of the gruff baker who forced his way in, and would not go. That such a contemptible nincompoop should dare to advise her father to be practical! The cleverest man in the world—advise him to be practical; as if, indeed, he was not practical and hard-working to the very utmost.

To her it was a bitter insult. The pencil trembled in her hand.

But what shook it most of all was anxiety about her mother. Ever since the bailiff's intrusion Mrs. Iden had seemed so unsettled. Sometimes she would come downstairs after the rest had retired, and sit by the dying fire for hours alone, till Iden chanced to wake, and go down for her.

Once she went out of doors very late, leaving the front door wide open, and Amaryllis found her at midnight wandering in an aimless way among the ricks.

At such times she had a glazed look in her eyes, and did not seem to see what she gazed at. At others she would begin to cry without cause, and gave indications of hysteria. The nervous Flamma family were liable to certain affections of that kind, and Amaryllis feared lest her mother's system had been overstrained by these continual worries.

Poor woman! she had, indeed, been worried enough to have shaken the strongest; and, having nothing stolid in her nature, it pressed upon her.

After awhile these attacks seemed to diminish, and Amaryllis hoped that nothing would come of it, but it left her in a state of extreme anxiety lest some fresh trouble should happen to renew the strain.

When she thought of her mother she could not draw—the sound of her shuffling, nervous footstep on the landing or the path outside under the window stopped her at once. These things disheartened her a thousand times more than the returned sketches the postman was always bringing.

On butter-making mornings, once a week, there was always a great to-do; Mrs. Iden, like nervous people, was cross and peevish when she was exceptionally busy, and clapper-clawed Iden to some purpose. It chanced that Amaryllis one day was just opening an envelope and taking out a returned drawing, when Iden entered, angry and fresh from Mrs. Iden's tongue, and, seeing the letter, began to growl:—

"Better drow that there fool stuff in the vire, and zee if you can't help your mother. Better do zummat to be some use on. Pity as you wasn't a boy chap to go out and yarn summat. Humph! humph!" growl, mutter, growl. "Drow" was local for throw, "summat" for something, "yarn" for earn. Unless I give you a vocabulary you may not be able to follow him.

The contemptuous allusion to her sketches as fool stuff, contrasted with the benefit and advantage of earning something— something real and solid—hit the artist very hard. That was the thought that troubled her so much, and paralysed her imagination. They were unsaleable—she saw the worthlessness of them far more than Iden. They were less in value than the paper on which they were traced; fool stuff, fit for the fire only.

That was the very thought that troubled her so, and Iden hit the nail home with his rude speech. That was the material view; unless a thing be material, or will fetch something material, it is good for the fire only.

So it came about that the portfolio was pushed aside, and dust gathered on it, and on the pencils, and the india-rubber, and in the little box of vine charcoal. Amaryllis having arranged her violets in the tumbler of water in the window niche, sat down at the table and leant her head on her hand, and tried to think what she could do, as she had thought these many, many days.

The drawings were so unreal, and a sovereign so real. Nothing in all the world at these moments seemed to her to be so good and precious as the round disk of gold which rules everything. The good that she could do with it—with just one of those golden disks!

Did you ever read Al Hariri? That accomplished scholar, the late Mr. Chenery (of The Times), translated twenty-six of his poems from the Arabic, and added most interesting notes. This curious book is a fusion of the Arabian Nights, Ecclesiastes, and Rabelais. There is the magical unexpectedness of the Arabian Nights, the vanity of vanities, all is vanity, of the Preacher, and the humour of the French satirist. Wisdom is scattered about it; at one moment you acknowledge a great thought, the next you are reproached for a folly, and presently laugh at a deep jest.

Al Hariri has a bearing upon Amaryllis, because he sang of the dinar, the Arabian sovereign, the double-faced dinar, the reverse and the obverse, head and tail, one side giving everything good, and the other causing all evil. For the golden disk has two sides, and two Fates belong to it. First he chants its praises:—

How noble is that yellow one, whose yellowness is pure,
Which traverses the regions, and whose journeying is afar.
Told abroad are its fame and repute:
Its lines are set as the secret sign of wealth;
Its march is coupled with the success of endeavours;
Its bright look is loved by mankind,
As though it had been molten of their hearts.
By its aid whoever has got it in his purse assails boldly,
Though kindred be perished or tardy to help.
Oh! charming are its purity and brightness;
Charming are its sufficiency and help.
How many a ruler is there whose rule has been perfected by it!
How many a sumptuous one is there whose grief, but for it, would be endless!
How many a host of cares has one charge of it put to flight!
How many a full moon has a sum of it brought down!
How many a one, burning with rage, whose coal is flaming,
Has it been secretly whispered to and then his anger has softened.
How many a prisoner, whom his kin had yielded,
Has it delivered, so that his gladness has been unmingled.
Now by the Truth of the Lord whose creation brought it forth,
Were it not for His fear, I should say its power is supreme.

The sovereign, our dinar, does it not answer exactly to this poem of the Arabian written in the days of the Crusades! It is yellow, it is pure, it travels vast distances, and is as valuable in India as here, it is famous and has a reputation, the inscription on it is the mark of its worth, it is the sinew of war, the world loves its brightness as if it was coined from their hearts, those who have it in their purses are bold, it helps every one who has it, it banishes all cares, and one might say, were it not for fear of the Lord, that the sovereign was all mighty.

All mighty for good as it seemed to Amaryllis thinking in her garret, leaning her head on her hand, and gazing at her violets; all mighty for good—if only she could get the real solid, golden sovereign!

But the golden coin has another side—the obverse—another Fate, for evil, clinging to it, and the poet, changing his tone, thunders:—

Ruin on it for a deceiver and insincere,
The yellow one with two faces like a hypocrite!
It shows forth with two qualities to the eye of him that looks on it,

The adornment of the loved one, the colour of the lover.
Affection for it, think they who judge truly,
Tempts men to commit that which shall anger their Maker.
But for it no thief's right hand were cut off;
Nor would tyranny be displayed by the impious;
Nor would the niggardly shrink from the night-farer;
Nor would the delayed claimant mourn the delay of him that withholds;
Nor would men call to God from the envious who casts at them.
Moreover the worst quality that it possesses
Is that it helps thee not in straits,
Save by fleeing from thee like a runaway slave.
Well done he who casts it away from a hilltop,
And who, when it whispers to him with the whispering of a lover,
Says to it in the words of the truth-speaking, the veracious,
"I have no mind for intimacy with thee,—begone!"

"The worst quality that it possesses" remains to this day, and could Amaryllis have obtained the sovereign, still it would only have helped her by passing from her, from her hand to that of the creditor's, fleeing like a runaway slave.

But Amaryllis surrounded with the troubles of her father and mother, saw only the good side of the golden sovereign, only that it was all powerful to bless.

How unnatural it seems that a girl like this, that young and fresh and full of generous feelings as she was, her whole mind should perforce be taken up with the question of money; an unnatural and evil state of things.

It seems to me very wicked that it should be so.

CHAPTER XXV

THOUGH the portfolio was pushed aside and dust had gathered on the table, except where her arm touched it, Amaryllis came daily, and often twice a day, to her flowers to pray.

From the woods she brought the delicate primrose opening on the mossy bank among the grey ash-stoles; the first tender green leaflet of hawthorn coming before the swallow; the garden crocus from the grass of the garden; the first green spikelet from the sward of the meadow; the beautiful white wild violets gathered in the sunlit April morning while the nightingale sang.

With these she came to pray each day, at the window-niche. After she had sat awhile at the table that morning, thinking, she went and knelt at the window with her face in her hands; the scent of the violets filled her hair.

Her prayer was deeper than words and was not put in language, but came rushing through her heart;—"That her dear mother might not suffer any more, that the strain of ceaseless trouble might be removed from her mind, that peace and rest might come to her in her old age. Let her step become firm, and the nervousness depart, and her eyes shine like they used to, so clear and bright, and do not let the grey hairs show more than they do now, or increase in number. Let her smile and be happy and talk cheerfully, and take an interest in the house and all the order of household things, and also see and understand that her husband meant to please her, even in such a little thing as splitting up useful wood for the fire, that he intended to please her, and that she might not misunderstand him any more. He intended to be kind in many ways, but misfortune had blinded her, and she took things the wrong way. And give her more change and friends to ask her out from home on visits, so that she might be amused, and make them come to see her and pass the time in contentment. Give her also enough money to buy good clothes so as to look nice as she ought to do, and if possible a conveyance of some kind—not a grand carriage, she did not wish for that—but a conveyance to drive about now and then, because she was not so strong as she used to be, and could not walk far. And let me, thought Amaryllis, let me be able to give her a watch, for other people have watches, and my mother has not got one, and it does seem so strange it should be so after all the hard work she has done. Let me, too, get her some nice things to eat, some fish and wine, for she cannot eat our plain bacon now every day, she has not got an appetite, and her teeth too are bad, and I should so like to give her a set of artificial teeth that her food might do her more good. But what I really want is that she may be happy, and be like my mother herself really is when she is herself. Give my father money enough to pay his creditors, for I know that though he is so quiet and says nothing, these debts are wearing him out, and I know he wishes to pay them, and does not willingly keep them waiting. He is so patient, and so good, and bears everything, I am sure no one was ever like him, and it is so dreadful to see him work, work, work, every day from five o'clock in the morning, and yet to be always worried with these debts and people that will not let him have peace one single day. Do, please, let him have less work to do,

100

it makes me miserable to see him in the rain, and he is not young now, and sometimes carrying such heavy things, great pieces of timber and large trusses of hay, and making his back ache digging. Surely it must soon be time for him to leave off working, he has done such a lot, and I do not think he can see quite so well as he used to, because he holds the paper so close to his eyes. Please let him leave off working soon now and have some rest and change, and go about with my mother, and when he is at home not have anything more to do than his garden, because he is so fond of that; let him love the flowers again as he used to, and plant some more, and have nothing harder to do than to gather the fruit from the trees he has planted. And let me get him some new books to read, because I know he is so fond of books; he has not had a new book for so long. Let him go to London and see people and things, and life, because I know he is full of ideas and thoughts though he works and digs, and that is what would do him good. Give him some money now at last, now he has worked all these years, forty years on this farm, and ever so much work before that; do give him some money at last. Do make my grandfather kinder to him and not so harsh for the rent, let him give the place to my father now, for it can be no use to him; let my father have it for his very own, and then I think he would be happy after all, he does so like to improve things and make them beautiful, and if it was his very own there is so much that he could do. That would be nice work and work that he would enjoy doing, and not just to get a few wretched shillings to pay other people. I am sure he would never be cross then, and he would be so kind to my mother, and kind and good to everybody. There is nobody like him, as you know, in this place; they are not clever like him, and good to the labouring men and their families like he is (and so is my mother too); they are so rough, and so unkind and stupid; I do not mean anything against them, but they are not like he is. And if you were to help him he would soon help the poor people and give them food and more wages; you know how good he is in his heart. And he would do it, not because other people should praise him, but because he would like to do it; if he does not go to church his heart is very true, and it is because he likes to be true and genuine, and not make any false show. Do, please, help him, and give him some money, and do, please, let him have this place for his very own, for I do so fear lest those who set my grandfather against him, should have a will made, so that my father should not have this house and land as he ought to do, as the son. He has made it so beautiful with trees, and brought the fresh spring water up to the house, and done so many clever things, and his heart is here, and it is home to him, and no other place could be like it. I think it would kill him not to have it, and for me, I should be so—I cannot tell, I should be so miserable if he did not, but I will not think of myself. There are so many things I know he wants to do if only he was not so worried with debts, and if he could feel it was his own land; he wants to plant a copse, and to make a pond by the brook, and have trout in it, and to build a wall by the rick-yard. Think how my dear father has worked all these years, and do help him now, and give him some money, and this place, and please do not let him grow any more grey than his hair is now, and save his eyes, for he is so fond of things that are beautiful, and please make my mother happy with him."

When Amaryllis rose from her knees her face was quite white, emotion had taken away her colour, and tears were thick on her cheek. She sat a little while by the table to recover herself, still thinking, and remembered that again last night she had dreamed the same dream about fire in the thatch. Somehow there seemed to be an alarm in the night, and they ran out of doors and found the corner of the roof on fire, over the window with the wire network instead of glass. It ran up from the corner towards the chimney, where the roof was mossy by the ridge. There was no flame, but a deep red seething heat, as if the straw burned inwardly, and was glowing like molten metal. Each straw seemed to lie in the furious heat, and a light to flicker up and down, as if it breathed fire. The thatch was very thick there, she knew, and recollected it quite well in her dream; Iden himself had laid on two thick coats in his time, and it was heavy enough before then. He talked about the thatching of it, because it was an argument with him that straw had a great power of endurance, and was equal to slates for lasting. This thickness, she saw, was the reason the fire did not blaze up quickly, and why, fortunately, it was slow in moving up the roof. It had not yet eaten through, so that there was no draught—once it got through, it would burn fast—if only they could put it out before then all might yet be saved. In the midst of her anxiety Iden came with the largest ladder in the rickyard, and mounted up, carrying a bucket of water. She tried to follow, holding on to the rungs of the ladder with one hand, and dragging up a heavy bucket with the other—the strain and effort to get up woke her.

This dream had happened to her so many times, and was so vivid and circumstantial—the fire seemed to glow in the thatch— that at last she began to dread lest it should come true. If it did not come true of the house itself, perhaps it would of the family, and of their affairs; perhaps it signified that the fire of debt, and poverty, and misfortune would burn them, as it were, to the ground. She tried to think whether in the dream they were getting the fire under before she woke, or whether they could not master it; it seemed dubious.

She did not tell her mother of the dream, afraid lest it might excite her again; nor could she tell Iden, who would have laughed at her.

Yet, though she knew it was but a dream, and dreams have ceased to come true, she did not like it; she felt uncertain, as if some indefinable danger was threatening round about. As she sat at the table she added to her prayer the supplication that the dear old house might not be burned down.

Soon afterwards she went down stairs, and on the lower flight paused, to listen to voices—not those of her mother and Iden— creditors, doubtless, come to cry aloud, "Pay me that thou owest!"— the very sum and total of religion. Her heart beat quicker—the voices came again, and she thought she recognized them, and that they were not those of creditors. She entered the sitting-room, and found that two visitors, from widely separated places, had arrived; one with a portmanteau, the other with an old, many-coloured carpet-bag. They were Amadis Iden, from Iden Court, over the Downs, the Court Idens, as they were called, and Alere Flamma, from London; the Flammas were carpet-bag people.

Her father was making them very welcome, after his wont, and they were talking of the house the Idens of yore had built in a lonely spot, expressly in order that they might drink, drink, drink undisturbed by their unreasonable wives.

CHAPTER XXVI

THEY talked on and on, these three, Iden, Amadis Iden, and Alere Flamma, with Amaryllis listening, from the end of April till near the end of May; till "a month passed away," and still they were talking. For there is nothing so good to the human heart as well agreed conversation, when you know that your companion will answer to your thought as the anvil meets the hammer, ringing sound to merry stroke; better than wine, better than sleep, like love itself—for love is agreement of thought—"God listens to those who pray to him; let us eat and drink, and think of nothing," says the

Arabian proverb. So they ate and drank—very moderate the drinking—and thought of nothing, and talked, which should be added to complete felicity. Not, of course, all of them always together, sometimes all four, sometimes Alere, Amadis, and Amaryllis, sometimes only the last two.

The round summer-house was their Parliament House whenever the east winds sank and the flowers shone forth like sunshine; as the sun shines when the clouds withdraw, so when the harsh east winds cease the May flowers immediately bloom and glow.

It was a large round house, properly builded of brick, as a summer-house should be—put not thy faith in lath work—and therefore dry and warm; to sit in it was like sitting in a shell, warm and comfortable, with a sea of meadow-grass, smooth and coloured, stretching in front, islanded about with oak, and elm, and ash.

The finches came to the boughs that hung over the ivy-grown thatch, and sang in the sycamore opposite the door, and in the apple-trees, whose bloom hung down almost to the ground.

These apple-trees, which Iden had planted, flung sackfuls of bloom at his feet. They poured themselves out in abandoned, open-armed, spendthrift, wasteful—perfectly prodigal—quantities of rose-tinted petal; prodigal as a river which flows full to the brim, never questioning but what there will be plenty of water to follow.

Flowers, and trees, and grass, seemed to spring up wherever Iden set down his foot: fruit and flowers fell from the air down upon him. It was his genius to make things grow—like sunshine and shower; a sort of Pan, a half-god of leaves and boughs, and reeds and streams, a sort of Nature in human shape, moving about and sowing Plenty and Beauty.

One side of the summer-house was a thick holly-bush, Iden had set it there; he builded the summer-house and set the ivy; and the pippin at the back, whose bloom was white; the copper-birch near by; the great sycamore alone had been there before him, but he set a seat under it, and got woodbine to flower there; the drooping-ash he planted, and if Amaryllis stood under it when the tree was in full leaf you could not see her, it made so complete an arbour; the Spanish oak in the corner; the box hedge along the ha-ha parapet; the red currants against the red wall; the big peony yonder; the damsons and pear; the yellow honey-bush; all these, and this was but one square, one mosaic of the garden, half of it sward, too, and besides these there was the rhubarb-patch at one corner; fruit, flowers, plants, and herbs, lavender, parsley, which has a very pleasant green, growing in a thick bunch, roses, pale sage—read

Boccaccio and the sad story of the leaf of sage—ask Nature if you wish to know how many things more there were.

A place to eat and drink, and think of nothing in, listening to the goldfinches, and watching them carry up the moss, and lichen, and slender fibres for their nest in the fork of the apple; listening to the swallows as they twittered past, or stayed on the sharp, high top of the pear tree; to the vehement starlings, whistling and screeching like Mrs. Iden herself, on the chimneys; chaffinches "chink, chink," thrushes, distant blackbirds, who like oaks; "cuckoo, cuckoo," "crake, crake," buzzing and burring of bees, coo of turtle-doves, now and then a neigh, to remind you that there were horses, fulness and richness of musical sound; a world of grass and leaf, humming like a hive with voices.

When the east wind ceases, and the sun shines above, and the flowers beneath, "a summer's day in lusty May," then is the time an Interlude in Heaven.

And all this, summer-house and all, had dropped out of the pocket of Iden's ragged old coat.

There was a magic power of healing in the influences of this place which Iden had created. Both Amadis and Alere Flamma had already changed for the better.

That morning when Amaryllis had found them, just arrived, the one with a portmanteau, and the other with a carpet-bag, they were both pale to the last degree of paleness.

Three years had gone by since Amadis had stayed at Coombe Oaks before, when Amaryllis was thirteen and he eighteen; fine romps they had then, a great girl, and a great boy, rowing on the water, walking over the hills, exploring the woods; Amadis shooting and fishing, and Amaryllis going with him, a kind of gamekeeper page in petticoats. They were of the same stock of Idens, yet no relations; he was of the older branch, Amaryllis of the younger.

She had grown into a woman; Amadis Iden into a man.

Sadly, indeed, he had altered. Looking at him, she could scarce believe he was the same; so pale, so thin, so drooping, and fireless—the spark of life sunk into the very ashes. He sat at the dinner-table that morning like a ghost. He was convalescent from low fever: that dread disease which has taken the place of ague in the country. At one time it was ague; in these times it is low fever.

At Coombe Oaks they had heard of his illness in a far-off way, but had received no distinct particulars, for the news came in a roundabout way by word of mouth, country-folk never write. The distance between the two houses was less than ten miles, and might as well have been five hundred for all the communication.

So that the ghastly paleness of his face came upon her as a

spectre in daylight. You could see at a glance what was wrong—the vital energy had been sapped; as a tree fades without a branch broken, or bark scored, fades and withers from the lack of the mysterious force which brings forth fresh leaves, so he drooped in his chair. The body—the tree—was there, but the life was not in it.

Alere Flamma, aged forty-nine, or nearly, was pale from other causes, and it was a different kind of paleness; not bloodlessness, like Amadis, but something lacking in the blood, a vitiated state. Too much Fleet Street, in short; too much of the Oracle—Pantagruel's Oracle of the Bottle.

His hands shook as he held his knife and fork—oddly enough, the hands of great genius often do shake; now and then when he put his glass to his lips, his teeth snapped on it, and chinked.

It seemed curious that such puffy, shaky hands could hold a pencil, and draw delicate lines without a flaw.

Many who never resort to the Oracle have hands that tremble nearly as much—the nervous constitution—and yet execute artists' work of rare excellence.

Alere's constitution, the Flamma constitution, naturally nervous, had been shaken as with dynamite by the bottle, and the glass chinked against his teeth. Every two or three years, when he felt himself toppling over like a tree half sawn through, Alere packed his carpet-bag, and ran down to Coombe Oaks. When the rats began to run up the wall as he sat at work in broad daylight, Alere put his slippers into his carpet-bag and looked out some collars.

In London he never wore a collar, only a bright red scarf round his neck; the company he kept would have shunned him—they would have looked him up and down disdainfully:—"Got a collar on—had no breakfast." They would have scornfully regarded him as no better than a City clerk, the class above all others scorned by those who use tools.

"Got a collar on—had no breakfast." The City clerk, playing the Masher on thirty shillings a week, goes without food to appear the gentleman.

Alere, the artist, drank with the men who used hammer, and file, or set up type—a godless set, ye gods, how godless, these setters up of type at four o'clock in the morning; oysters and stout at 4 a.m.; special taverns they must have open for them—open before Aurora gleams in the east—Oh! Fleet Street, Fleet Street, what a place it is!

By no possible means could Alere work himself into a dress-coat.

Could he have followed the celebrated advice—"You put on a

dress-coat and go into society"—he would soon have become a name, a fame, a taker of big fees, a maker of ten thousand yearly.

To a man who could draw like Alere, possessed, too, of the still rarer talent—the taste to see what to draw—there really is no limit in our days; for as for colour, you do not require a genius for colour in an age of dinginess—why, the point, nowadays, is to avoid colour, and in a whole Academy you shall scarcely find as much as would tint a stick of sealing-wax.

"You put on a black coat and go into society"—that is the secret of commissions, and commissions are fortune. Nothing so clever in the way of advice has been sent forth as that remark. The great Tichborne said something about folk that had money and no brains, and folk that had brains but no money; and they as has no brains ought to be so managed as to supply money to those who had. But even the greatness of the great Tichborne's observation falls into insignificance before Chesterfield in one sentence: "Put on a black coat and go into society."

What are the sayings of the seven wise men of Greece compared to that?

CHAPTER XXVII

BY no possible means could Alere Flamma work himself into a dress coat. The clubs, the houses of the great, the mutual admiration dinners—those great institutions of the day—were all closed to him because of the Dress Coat.

If he had really desired to enter, of course he would have squeezed into the evening monkey-skin somehow; but, in truth, Alere did not want to enter.

Inside he might have finished a portrait a month at a thousand guineas—twelve portraits per annum equals twelve thousand guineas a year; you see I am looking up the multiplication table, preparatory to going into the tallow trade.

What he actually did was to make designs for book-covers— magnificent book-covers that will one day fetch their weight in bank-notes—manipulating a good deal of it himself—"tooling"—for

107

the libraries of noble connoisseurs. They were equal to anything ever done in Paris.

For a week's work—say half-an-hour a day—he got perhaps about ten pounds. With the ten pounds he was satisfied—ten pounds represents a good deal of brandy, or stout, or even wine, about as much as one man can manage at a bout; besides tobacco, the gallery at the theatre, and innumerable trifles of that kind. Ten pounds represents a good deal of street life.

Sometimes he drew—and engraved—illustrations for books, being as clever with the engraver's tools as with the pencil; sometimes he cut out those odd, fantastic "initials," "ornaments," "finials," which are now so commonly seen in publications, catching the classical grotesque of the Renaissance to perfection, and deceiving the experienced; sometimes he worked in the press-room in the House of Flamma, Fleet Street, pulling artists' proofs, or printing expensively illustrated volumes—numbered, and the plates destroyed—actual manual work, in his shirt sleeves.

He could stop when he liked and take a swig of stout. That was the Alere style.

Smoking was forbidden in the old House of Flamma because of the worm-eaten beams, the worm-eaten rafters and staircase, the dusty, decayed bookshelves, the dry, rotten planks of the floor, the thin wooden partitions, all ready to catch fire at the mere sight of a match. Also because of the piles of mouldy books which choked the place, and looked fit for nothing but a bonfire, but which were worth thousands of pounds; the plates and lithographic stones, artists' proofs, divers and sundry Old Masters in a room upstairs, all easily destructible.

But Alere, being a son of the house, though not in command, did not choose to be amenable to rules and orders in fact, in fiction he was. He smoked and kept the glue-pot ready on the stove; if a certain step was known to be approaching the pipe was thrust out of sight, and some dry glue set melting, the powerful incense quite hiding the flavour of tobacco. A good deal of dry glue is used in London in this way.

If I could but write the inside history of Fleet Street, I should be looked upon as the most wonderful exponent of human life that had ever touched a pen. Balzac—whom everybody talks of and nobody has read, because the discrimination of Paternoster Row has refused him a translation till quite lately—Zola, who professes to be realistic, who is nothing if not realistic, but whose writings are so curiously crude and merely skim the surface; even the great Hugo, who produced the masterpiece of all fiction, Les Misérables; all three of them, the entire host of manuscript-makers, I am sure I could vanquish them all, if I could only write the inside life of Fleet Street.

Not in any grace of style or sweeping march of diction, but just pencil-jotted in the roughest words to hand, just as rich and poor, well-dressed ladies and next-door beggars are bundled into a train, so, without choice of language, but hustling the first words anyhow, as it were, into the first compartment. If I could only get Alere to tell me all he had seen in Fleet Street, and could just jot it down on the margin of a stained newspaper, all the world would laugh and weep. For such things do go on in Fleet Street as no man has written yet.

If only Victor Hugo were alive and young again!

Alere liked pulling off the proofs in his shirt-sleeves, swigging his stout, smoking on the sly, working with all the genius of an inspired mechanic one moment and dropping into absolute idleness the next, spending infinite pains in finishing one bit of work, as if his very life depended on the smoothing of an edge of paper, putting off the next till the end of the month, pottering, sleeping, gossiping, dreaming over old German works, and especially dreaming over Goethe, humming old German songs—for he had been a great traveller—sometimes scrawling a furious Mazzinian onslaught in a semi-Nihilist foreign print, collecting stray engravings, wandering hither and thither.

Alere Flamma, artist, engraver, bookbinder, connoisseur, traveller, printer, Republican, conspirator, sot, smoker, dreamer, poet, kind-hearted, good-natured, prodigal, shiftless, man of Fleet Street, carpet-bag man, gentleman shaken to pieces.

He worked in his shirt-sleeves and drank stout, but nothing vulgar had ever been recorded against Alere Flamma. He frequented strong company—very strong meat—but no vile word left his lips.

There was a delicacy in all his ways in the midst of the coarsest surroundings, just as he appeared in the press-room among the printer's ink in the whitest of clean shirt-sleeves, fit to wear with the abhorred dress-coat.

In his rooms at his lodgings there were literally hundreds of sketches, done on all sorts and sizes of paper, from the inside of an envelope hastily torn open to elephant. The bureau was full of them, crammed in anyhow, neither sorted nor arranged; nothing, of course, could be found if it was wanted. The drawers of the bookcase—it was his own furniture—were full of them; the writing-table drawer; a box in one corner; some were on the mantelpiece smoked and gritty; some inside his books, most of which were interleaved in this manner; literally hundreds of sketches, the subjects as numerous and varied.

Views in English country lanes, views on the Danube, bands playing in band-loving Vienna, old Highgate Archway, studies from Canterbury Cathedral, statuary in the Louvre, ships battling with the north wind in the North Sea—a savage fight between sail and gale—horses in the meadow, an aged butler, a boy whipping a top, charcoal-burners in the Black Forest, studies from the nude—Parisian models, Jewesses, almost life-size, a drayman heaving up a huge tankard, overshadowing his face like Mount Atlas turned over his thumb, designs to illustrate classical mythology, outlines expressing the ideas of Goethe—outlines of Marguerite and Faust among the roses—"He loves me; he loves me not," big-armed Flemish beauties with breasts as broad as the Zuyder-Zee was deep in the song, roofs of Nuremberg, revolutionary heroes charging their muskets in the famous year '48, when Alere had a bullet through his hat, in Vienna, I think; no end to them.

Sometimes when Alere had done no work for a month or two, and his ten pounds were spent, if he wanted a few guineas he would take a small selection of these round to the office of a certain illustrated paper; the Editor would choose, and hand over the money at once, well aware that it was ready money his friend needed. They were not exactly friends—there are no friends in London, only acquaintances—but a little chummy, because the Editor himself had had a fiery youth, and they had met in sunny Wien. That was the only paper that ever got sketches out of Alere.

If only Alere would have gone and sketched what he was asked to sketch! Ah! there is the difference; he could not do it, his nature would not let him; he could draw what he saw with his own eyes, but not what other people wanted him to see. A merry income he might have made if he would only have consented to see what other eyes—common, vulgar eyes—wanted to see, and which he could so easily have drawn for them.

Out of these piles of varied sketches there were two kinds the Editor instantly snapped at: the one was wild flowers, the other little landscape bits.

Wild flowers were his passion. They were to Flamma as Juliet to Romeo. Romeo's love, indeed, rushed up like straw on fire, a great blaze of flame; he perished in it as the straw; perhaps he might not have worshipped Juliet next year. Flamma had loved his wild flowers close upon forty years, ever since he could remember; most likely longer, for doubtless the dumb infant loved the daisies put in his chubby hand.

His passion they were still as he drew near fifty, and saw all things become commonplace. That is the saddest of thoughts—as we grow older the romance fades, and all things become commonplace.

110

Half our lives are spent in wishing for to-morrow, the other half in wishing for yesterday.

Wild flowers alone never become commonplace. The white wood-sorrel at the foot of the oak, the violet in the hedge of the vale, the thyme on the wind-swept downs, they were as fresh this year as last, as dear to-day as twenty years since, even dearer, for they grow now, as it were, in the earth we have made for them of our hopes, our prayers, our emotions, our thoughts.

Sketch-book upon sketch-book in Alere's room was full of wild flowers, drawn as he had found them in the lanes and woods at Coombe Oaks—by the footpaths, by the lake and the lesser ponds, on the hills—as he had found them, not formed into an artificial design, not torn up by the roots, or cut and posed for the occasion—exactly as they were when his eye caught sight of them. A difficult thing to do, but Alere did it.

In printing engravings of flowers the illustrated magazines usually make one of two mistakes; either the flower is printed without any surroundings or background, and looks thin, quite without interest, however cleverly drawn, or else it is presented with a heavy black pall of ink which dabs it out altogether.

These flowers the Editor bought eagerly, and the little landscapes. From a stile, beside a rick, through a gap in a hedge, odd, unexpected places, Alere caught views of the lake, the vale, the wood, groups of trees, old houses, and got them in his magical way on a few square inches of paper. They were very valuable for book illustration. They were absolutely true to nature and fact.

CHAPTER XXVIII

PERHAPS the reason Alere never took to colours was because of his inherent and unswerving truthfulness of character. Genuine to a degree, he could not make believe—could not deceive—could not masquerade in a dress-coat.

Now, most of the landscape-painting in vogue to-day is nature in a dress-coat.

In a whole saloon of water colours, in a whole Academy, or Grosvenor Gallery you shall hardly find three works that represent any real scene in the fields.

I have walked about the fields a good deal in my brief, fretful hour, yet I have never seen anything resembling the strange apparitions that are hung on these walls every spring. Apparitions—optical illusions, lit up with watery, greenish, ghastly, ghost-light—nothing like them on earth I swear, and I suspect not in Heaven or Hades.

Touched-up designs: a tree taken from one place, a brook from another, a house from another—and mixed to order, like a prescription by the chemist—xv. grs. grass, 3 dr. stile, iiij. grs. rustic bridge. Nature never plants—nature is no gardener—no design, no proportion in the fields.

Colours! Passing a gasworks perhaps you may have noticed that the surface of the water in the ditch by the roadside bears a greenish scum, a pale prismatic scum; this is the colour-box of modern landscape.

How horrible the fields would look if they wore such hues in reality as are accepted on canvas at the galleries! Imagine these canvas tints transferred to the sward, the woods, the hills, the streams, the sky! Dies iræ, dies illæ—it would, indeed, be an awful day, the Last Day of Doom, and we should need the curtain at Drury Lane drawn before our eyes to shut it out of sight.

There are some who can go near to paint dogs and horses, but a meadow of mowing grass, not one of them can paint that.

Many can draw nature—drawings are infinitely superior generally to the painting that follows; scarce one now paints real nature.

Alere could not squeeze his sketches into the dress-coat of sham colour for any sacred exhibition wall whatever.

One thing Alere never attempted to draw—a bird in flight. He recognized that it was impossible; his taste rejected every conventional attitude that has been used for the purpose; the descending pigeon, the Japanese skewered birds, the swallow skimming as heavily as a pillow. You cannot draw a bird in flight. Swallows are attempted oftenest, and done worst of all.

How can you draw life itself? What is life? you cannot even define it. The swallow's wing has the motion of life—its tremble—its wonderful delicacy of vibration—the instant change—the slip of the air;—no man will ever be able to draw a flying swallow.

At the feet of this Gamaliel of Fleet Street, Amaryllis had sat much, from time to time, when the carpet-bag was packed and Alere withdrew to his Baden-Baden—i.e., to Coombe Oaks and apple-bloom, singing finch, and wild-flowers.

There were no "properties" in Alere's room at his lodgings; no odd bits collected during his wanderings to come in useful some day as make-up, realistic rock work, as it were, in the picture. No gauntlets or breast-plates, scraps of old iron; no Turkish guns or yataghans, no stags' horns, china, or carvings to be copied some day into an illustration. No "properties."

No studio effects. The plaster bust that strikes the key and tones the visitors' mind to "Art," the etchings, the wall or panel s, the sliding curtains, the easels in the corner, the great portfolios—the well-known "effects" were absent.

A plain room, not even with a north light, plain old furniture, but not very old—not ostensibly ancient, somewhere about 1790 say—and this inherited and not purchased; Flamma cared not one atom for furniture, itself, old or new; dusty books everywhere, under the table, on the mantelpiece, beside the coal scuttle; heaps on chairs, quartos on the sofa, crowds more in his bedroom, besides the two bookcases and drawers; odd books most of them, Cornelius Agrippa, Le Petit Albert, French illustrated works, editions of Faust, music, for Flamma was fond of his many-keyed flute.

Great people once now and then called and asked to see Alere Flamma at the business place in Fleet Street; people with titles, curiously out of place, in the press-room, gold leaf on the floor, odour of printer's ink, dull blows of machinery, rotten planking, partitions pasted over with illustrations and stained with beer, the old place trembling as the engine worked; Flamma, in his shirt-sleeves, talking to "His Excellency."

Flamma's opinion, information he could give, things he knew; abroad they thought much of him.

Presents came occasionally—a boar's head from Germany; fine Havana cigars—Alere always had a supply of the best cigars and Turkish tobacco, a perennial stream of tobacco ran for him; English venison; once a curious dagger from Italy, the strangest present good-natured Alere could possibly have received!

Sometimes there came a pressing invitation from a noble connoisseur to his country seat; Flamma's views were wanted about the re-arrangement of the library, the re-binding of some treasure picked up in a cover all too poor for its value, the building of another wing, for the artist is the true architect, as the princes of Italy knew of old time. Till the artist is called in we shall never again see real architecture in the world. Did not Benvenuto design fortifications? Did not Michael Angelo build St. Peter's at Rome?

If my lord duke wants a palace he cannot have it till he calls in the artist, the Alere Flamma, to draw it for him; if my lord bishop needs a cathedral he cannot have it till he calls in the poet-draughtsman, till he goes to Alere Flamma.

Our so-called architects are mere surveyors, engineers,

educated bricklayers, men of hard straight ruler and square, mathematically accurate, and utterly devoid of feeling.

The princes of Italy knew better—they called in the poet and the painter, the dreamers to dream for them.

You call in your "practical" architect, and he builds you a brick box; not for a hundred thousand pounds in fees could he build you a palace or a cathedral.

The most ignorant of men are the "practical" people. It is meet and fitting that they should be worshipped and set on high. The calf worshipped of old was at least golden, and these are of lead.

But Alere could not go; he would do anything he was asked in this way; he would take infinite pains to please, but he could not leave Fleet Street for any mansion.

When a man once gets into Fleet Street he cannot get out.

Conventionally, I suppose, it would be the right thing to represent Alere as a great genius neglected, or as a genius destroyed by intemperance. The conventional type is so easy—so accepted—so popular; it would pay better, perhaps, to make him out a victim in some way.

He was not neglected, neither was he the victim of intemperance in the usual sense.

The way to fame and fortune had always been wide open to him; there were long intervals when he did not drink, nor did drink enfeeble his touch; it was not half so much to struggle against as the chest diseases from which professional men so often suffer; I believe if he had really tried or wished he could have conquered his vice altogether. Neither of these causes kept him from the foremost rank.

There was no ambition, and there was no business-avarice. So many who have no ideal are kept hard at work by the sheer desire of money, and thus spurred onward, achieve something approaching greatness. Alere did not care for money.

He could not get out of Fleet Street. Ten pounds was a large sum in the company he frequented; he did not want any more.

CHAPTER XXIX

SOMETHING in Fleet Street holds tight those who once come within its influence. The cerebellum of the world, the "grey matter" of the world's brain, lies somewhere thereabouts. The thoughts of our time issue thence, like the radiating spokes of a wheel, to all places of the earth. There you have touch of the throbbing pulse of the vast multitudes that live and breathe. Their ideas come from Fleet Street.

From the printing-press and the engraver's wood-block, the lithographic-stone, the etcher's plate, from book and magazine, periodical and pamphlet, from world-read newspaper.

From Fleet Street, the centre whence ideas flow outwards.

It is joyous to be in the flower-grown meads; it is sweet to be on the hill-top; delicious to feel the swell and the long roll of the hexameter of the seas; doubtless there is a wild rapture on the summit of the Himalayas; triumph in the heart of the African explorer at the river's source. But if once the mind has been dipped in Fleet Street, let the meads be never so sweet, the mountain-top never so exalted, still to Fleet Street the mind will return, because there is that other Mind, without whose sympathy even success is nothing—the Mind of the world.

I am, of course, thinking not only of the thoroughfare, Fleet Street, but of all that the printing-press means.

Alere was no leader of thought, but it was necessary to him to live and breathe in the atmosphere of thought—to feel the throb and swell around him—to be near the "grey matter" of the world's brain.

Once a man gets into Fleet Street he cannot get out. Flamma would not leave it for months of gilded idleness in any nobleman's mansion.

The flame must be fed. His name had some connection with the design of the Roman lamp on the splendid bindings of the books tooled in the House of Flamma. Alere Flammam—feed the flame. The flame of the mind must be fed.

Sad things happen on the stones of Fleet Street; if I could but get at it all to write the inside life of it, it would, indeed, be a book. Stone-cold poverty hovers about. The rich, living in the fool's paradise of money, think they know life, but they do not, for, as was said of the sea——

Only those who share its dangers
Comprehend its mystery.

115

Only those who have shared the struggle literally for bread—for a real, actual loaf—understand the dread realities of man's existence.

Let but a morsel of wood—a little splinter of deal, a curl of carpenter's shaving—lie in Fleet Street, and it draws to it the wretched human beasts as surely as the offal draws the beast of the desert to the camp. A morsel of wood in the streets that are paved with gold!

It is so valuable. Women snatch it up and roll it in their aprons, clasping it tightly, lest it should somehow disappear. Prowling about from street to street, mile after mile, they fill their aprons with these precious splinters of deal, for to those who are poor fuel is as life itself.

Even the wealthy, if they have once been ill, especially of blood-thinning diseases (as rheumatism), sometimes say they would rather go without food than coal. Rather emptiness than chill.

These women know where there are hoardings erected by builders, where shop-fronts are being rebuilt, where fires have taken place, where alterations are proceeding; they know them as the birds know the places where they are likely to find food, and visit them day by day for the scraps of wood and splinters that drop on the pavement.

Or they send their children, ragged urchins, battling for a knot of pine-wood.

The terror of frost to these creatures is great indeed. Frost is the King of Terrors to them—not Death; they sleep and live with death constantly, the dead frequently in the room with the living, and with the unborn that is near birth.

Alere's ten pounds helped them. The drunkard's wife knew that Flamma, the drinker, would certainly give her the silver in his pocket.

The ragged urchins, battling for a knot of pine-wood, knew that they could charm the pennies and the threepenny bits out of his waistcoat; the baked potatoes and the roasted chestnuts looked so nice on the street stove.

Wretched girls whose power of tempting had gone, and with it their means of subsistence, begged, and not in vain, of shaky Alere Flamma. There are many of these wretches in Fleet Street. There is no romance about them to attract the charity of the world.

Once a flower-girl, selling flowers without a licence in the street, was charged by the police. How this harshness to the flower-girl—the human representation of Flora—roused up sentiment in her behalf!

But not every starving girl has the fortune to rouse up

116

sentiment and to be fed. Their faces disfigured with eruptions, their thin shoulders, their dry, disordered hair—hair never looks nice unless soft with its natural oil—their dingy complexions, their threadbare shawls, tempt no one. They cannot please, therefore they must starve.

The good turn from them with horror—Are they not sin made manifest? The trembling hand of Alere fed them.

Because the boys bawl do you suppose they are happy? It is curious that people should associate noise with a full stomach. The shoeblack boys, the boys that are gathered into institutions and training ships, are expected to bawl and shout their loudest at the annual fêtes when visitors are present. Your bishops and deans forthwith feel assured that their lives are consequently joyous.

Why then do they set fire to training ships? Why do they break out of reformatory institutions? Bawling is not necessarily happiness. Yet fatuous fools are content if only they can hear a good uproar of bawling.

I have never walked up Fleet Street and the Strand yet without seeing a starving woman and child. The children are indeed dreadful; they run unguarded and unwatched out of the side courts into the broader and more lively Strand—the ceaseless world pushes past—they play on the pavement unregarded. Hatless, shoeless, bound about with rags, their faces white and scarred with nameless disease, their eyes bleared, their hair dirty; little things, such as in happy homes are sometimes set on the table to see how they look.

How can people pass without seeing them?

Alere saw them, and his hand went to his waistcoat pocket.

The rich folk round about this great Babylon of Misery, where cruel Want sits on the Seven Hills—make a cartoon of that!—the rich folk who receive hundreds on the turn of a stock, who go to the Bank of England on dividend days—how easily the well-oiled doors swing open for them!—who dwell in ease and luxury at Sydenham, at Norwood, at Surbiton, at Streatham, at Brighton, at Seven-oaks, wherever there is pure air, have distinguished themselves lately in the giving of alms, ordained by the Lord whom they kneel before each Sunday, clad in silk, scarlet, and fine linen, in their cushioned pews.

They have established Homes for Lost Dogs and Homes for Lost Cats, neither of which are such nuisances as human beings.

In the dog institution they have set up an apparatus specially designed by one of the leading scientific men of the age. The dogs that are not claimed in a certain time, or that have become diseased—like the human nuisances—are put into this apparatus, into a comfortable sort of chamber, to gnaw their last bone. By-and-by, a scientific vapour enters the chamber, and breathing this, the animal falls calmly to death, painlessly poisoned in peace.

Seven thousand dogs were thus happily chloroformed "into eternity" in one season. Jubilant congratulations were exchanged at the success of the apparatus. Better than shooting, drowning, hanging, vivisection, or starvation!

Let a dog die in peace. Is not this an age of humanity indeed? To sell all you have and give to the poor was nothing compared to this. We have progressed since Anno Domini I. We know better how to do it now.

Alere did not seem to trouble himself much about the dogs; he saw so much of the human nuisances.

What a capital idea it would be to set up an apparatus like this in the workhouses and in conjunction with the hospitals!

Do you know, thoughtless, happy maiden, singing all the day, that one out of every five people who die in London, die in the workhouse or the hospital?

Eighty-two thousand people died in London in 1882, and of these, fourteen thousand expired in the workhouses, and six thousand in hospitals!

Are not these ghastly figures? By just setting up a few Apparatuses, see what an immense amount of suffering would be saved, and consider what a multitude of human nuisances would he "moved on!"

The poor have a saying that none live long after they have been in a certain hospital. "He's been in that hospital—he won't live long." They carry out such wonderful operations there—human vivisections, but strictly painless, of course, under chloroform—true Christian chopping-up—still the folk do not live long when they come out.

Why not set up the Apparatus? But a man must not die in peace. Starvation is for human nuisances.

These rich folk dwelling round about the great Babylon of Misery, where Want sits on the Seven Hills, have also distinguished themselves by yet another invention. This is the organization of alms. Charity is so holy we will not leave it to chance—to the stray penny—we will organize it. The system is very simple: it is done by ticket. First you subscribe a few shillings to some organization, with its secretary, its clerks, its offices, board-room, and "machinery." For this you receive tickets.

If a disagreeable woman with a baby in her arms, or a ragged boy, or a maimed man asks you for a "copper," you hand him a ticket. This saves trouble and responsibility.

The beggar can take the ticket to the "office" and get his case "investigated." After an inquiry, and an adjournment for a week; another inquiry, and another adjournment for a week; a third inquiry, and a third adjournment, then, if he be of high moral character and highly recommended, he may get his dinner.

One great advantage is conspicuous in this system: by no possible means can you risk giving a penny to a man not of high moral character, though he be perishing of starvation.

If a man asks for bread, will ye give him a stone? Certainly not; give him a ticket.

They did not understand how to do things in Judea Anno Domini I.

This organization of charity saves such a lot of money: where people used to give away five pounds they now pay five shillings.

Nothing like saving money. And, besides, you walk about with a clear conscience. No matter how many maimed men, or disagreeable women, or ragged boys you see, you can stroll on comfortably and never think about them; your charity is organized.

If the German thinkers had not found out twenty years ago that there was no Devil, one would be inclined to ascribe this spurious, lying, false, and abominable mockery to the direct instigation of a Satan.

The organization of charity! The very nature of charity is spontaneousness.

You should have heard Alere lash out about this business; he called it charity suppression.

Have you ever seen London in the early winter morning, when the frost lies along the kerb, just melting as the fires are lit; cold, grey, bitter, stony London?

Whatever can morning seem like to the starved and chilly wretches who have slept on the floor, and wake up to frost in Fleet Street?

The pavements are covered with expectoration, indicating the chest diseases and misery that thousands are enduring. But I must not write too plainly; it would offend.

CHAPTER XXX

APRINTER in the office crawled under the bed of the machine to replace something—a nut that had dropped; it was not known that he was there; the crank came round and crushed him against the brickwork. The embrace of iron is death.

Alere fed his helpless children, and apprenticed them when they were old enough.

Ten pounds was enough for him—without ambition, and without business-avarice; ten pounds was enough for his Fleet Street life.

It was not only the actual money he gave away, but the kindness of the man. Have you ever noticed the boys who work in printing-offices?—their elbows seem so sharp and pointed, bony, and without flesh. Instead of the shirt-sleeve being turned up, it looks as if the pointed elbow had thrust its way through.

He always had something for them;—a plate of beef, soup, beer to be shared, apples, baked potatoes, now and then half-a-dozen mild cigars. Awful this, was it not? Printers' boys will smoke; they had better have Flamma's fine tobacco than the vile imitation they buy.

They always had a tale for him; either their mothers, or sisters, or some one was in trouble; Flamma was certain to do something, however little might be within his power. At least he went to see.

Had a man an income of a million he could not relieve the want of London; the wretch relieved to-day needs again to-morrow. But Alere went to see.

Ten pounds did much in the shaky hands of a man without ambition, and without business-avarice, who went to see the unfortunate.

His own palsied mother, at the verge of life, looked to Alere for all that the son can do for the parent. Other sons seemed more capable of such duty; yet it invariably fell upon Alere. He was the Man. And for those little luxuries and comforts that soothe the dull hours of trembling age she depended entirely upon him.

So you see the ten-pound notes that satisfied him were not all spent in drink.

But alas! once now and then the rats began to run up the wall in broad daylight, and foolish Alere, wise in this one thing, immediately began to pack his carpet-bag. He put in his collars, his slippers, his sketch-books and pencils, some of his engraving tools, and a few blocks of boxwood, his silver-mounted flute, and a book for Amaryllis. He packed his carpet-bag and hastened away to his Baden-Baden, to Coombe Oaks, his spa among the apple-bloom, the song of finches, and rustle of leaves.

They sat and talked in the round summer-house in Iden's garden, with the summer unfolding at their knees; Amaryllis, Amadis, Iden, and Flamma.

By Flamma's side there stood a great mug of the Goliath ale, and between his lips there was a long churchwarden pipe.

The Goliath ale was his mineral water; his gaseous, alkaline, chalybeate liquor; better by far than Kissingen, Homburg, Vichy; better by far than mud baths and hot springs. There is no medicine in nature, or made by man, like good ale. He who drinks ale is strong.

The bitter principle of the aromatic hops went to his nervous system, to the much-suffering liver, to the clogged and weary organs, bracing and stimulating, urging on, vitalizing anew.

The spirit drawn from the joyous barley warmed his heart; a cordial grown on the sunny hill-side, watered with dew and sweet rain, coloured by the light, a liquor of sunshine, potable sunbeam.

Age mingling hops and barley in that just and equitable proportion, no cunning of hand, no science can achieve, gave to it the vigour of years, the full manhood of strength.

There was in it an alchemic power analysis cannot define. The chemist analyzes, and he finds of ten parts, there are this and there are that, and the residue is "volatile principle," for which all the dictionaries of science have no explanation.

"Volatile principle"—there it is, that is the secret. That is the life of the thing; by no possible means can you obtain that volatile principle—that alchemic force—except contained in genuine old ale.

Only it must be genuine, and it must be old; such as Iden brewed.

The Idens had been famous for ale for generations.

By degrees Alere's hand grew less shaky; the glass ceased to chink against his teeth; the strong, good ale was setting his Fleet Street liver in order.

You have "liver," you have "dyspepsia," you have "kidneys," you have "abdominal glands," and the doctor tells you you must take bitters, i.e., quassia, buchu, gentian, cascarilla, calumba; aperients and diluents, podophyllin, taraxacum, salts; physic for the nerves and blood, quinine, iron, phosphorus; this is but the briefest outline of your draughts and preparations; add to it for various purposes, liquor arsenicalis, bromide of potassium, strychnia, belladonna.

Weary and disappointed, you turn to patent medicines—American and French patent physic is very popular now—and find the same things precisely under taking titles, enormously advertised.

It is a fact that nine out of ten of the medicines compounded are intended to produce exactly the same effects as are caused by a few glasses of good old ale. The objects are to set the great glands in motion, to regulate the stomach, brace the nerves, and act as a tonic and cordial; a little ether put in to aid the digestion of the compound. This is precisely what good old ale does, and digests itself very comfortably. Above all things, it contains the volatile principle, which the prescriptions have not got.

Many of the compounds actually are beer, bittered with quassia instead of hops; made nauseous in order that you may have faith in them.

"Throw physic to the dogs," get a cask of the true Goliath, and "drenk un down to the therd hoop."

Long before Alere had got to the first hoop the rats ceased to run up the wall, his hand became less shaky, he began to play a very good knife and fork at the bacon and Iden's splendid potatoes; by-and-by he began to hum old German songs.

But you may ask, how do you know, you're not a doctor, you're a mere story-spinner, you're no authority? I reply that I am in a position to know much more than a doctor.

How can that be?

Because I have been a Patient. It is so much easier to be a doctor than a patient. The doctor imagines what his prescriptions are like and what they will do; he imagines, but the Patient knows.

CHAPTER XXXI

SOME noble physicians have tried the effect of drugs upon themselves in order to advance their art; for this they have received Gold Medals, and are alluded to as Benefactors of Mankind.

I have tried the effects of forty prescriptions upon My Person. With the various combinations, patent medicines, and so forth, the total would, I verily believe, reach eighty drugs.

Consequently, it is clear I ought to receive eighty gold medals.

I am a Benefactor eighty times multiplied; the incarnation of virtue; a sort of Buddha, kiss my knees, ye slaves!

I have a complaisant feeling as I walk about that I have thus done more good than any man living.

I am still very ill.

The curious things an invalid is gravely recommended to try! One day I was sitting in that great cosmopolitan museum, the waiting-room at Charing Cross station, wearily glancing from time to time at the clock, and reckoning how long it would be before I could get home. There is nothing so utterly tiring to the enfeebled as an interview with a London physician. So there I sat, huddled of a heap, quite knocked up, and, I suppose, must have coughed from time to time. By-and-by, a tall gentleman came across the room and sat down beside me. "I hope I don't intrude," said he, in American accents. "I was obliged to come and speak to you—you look bad. I hate to hear anybody cough." He put an emphasis on hate, a long-drawn nasal haate, hissing it out with unmeasured ferocity. "I haate to hear anybody cough. Now I should like to tell you how to cure it, if you don't mind."

"By all means—very interesting," I replied.

"I was bad at home, in the States," said he. "I was on my back four years with a cough. I couldn't do anything—couldn't help myself; four years, and I got down to eighty-seven pounds. That's a fact, I weighed eighty-seven pounds."

"Very little," I said, looking him over; he was tall and broad-shouldered, not very thick, a square-set man.

"I tried everything the doctors recommended—it was no use; they had to give me up. At last a man cured me; and how do you think he did it?"

"Can't think—should much like to know."

"Crude petroleum," said the American. "That was it. Crude petroleum! You take it just as it comes from the wells; not refined, mind. Just crude. Ten drops on a bit of sugar three times a day, before meals. Taste it? No, not to speak of; you don't mind it after a little while. I had in a ten-gallon keg. I got well. I got up to two hundred and fifty pounds. That's true. I got too fat, had to check it. But I take the drops still, if I feel out of sorts. Guess I'm strong enough now. Been all over Europe."

I looked at him again; certainly, he did appear strong enough.

"But you Britishers won't try anything, I suppose, from the States, now."

I hastened to assure him I had no prejudice of that sort—if it would cure me, it might come from anywhere.

"You begin with five drops," he said, solemnly. "Or three, if you like, and work up to ten. It soon gets easy to take. You'll soon pick up. But I doubt if you'll get a keg of the crude oil in this country; you'll have to send over for it. I haate to hear anybody cough"—and so we parted.

He was so much in earnest, that if I had egged him on, I verily believe he would have got the keg for me himself. It seemed laughable at the time; but I don't laugh now. I almost think that good-natured American was right; he certainly meant well.

Crude petroleum! Could anything be more nauseous? But probably it acts as a kind of cod-liver oil. Sometimes I wish I had tried it. Like him, I hate to hear anybody cough! Better take a ten-gallon keg of petroleum.

Alere's crude petroleum was the Goliath ale, and he had hardly begun to approach the first hoop, when, as I tell you, he was heard to hum old German songs; it was the volatile principle.

Songs about the Pope and the Sultan

> But yet he's not a happy man,
> He must obey the Alcoran,
> He dares not touch one drop of wine,
> I'm glad the Sultan's lot's not mine.

Songs about the rat that dwelt in the cellar, and fed on butter till he raised a paunch that would have done credit to Luther; songs about a King in Thule and the cup his mistress gave him, a beautiful old song that, none like it—

> He saw it fall, he watched it fill,
> And sink deep, deep into the main;
> Then sorrow o'er his eyelids fell,
> He never drank a drop again.

Or his thought slipped back to his school-days, and beating the seat in the summer-house with his hand for time, Alere ran on:—

> Horum scorum suntivorum,
> Harum scarum divo,
> Tag-rag, merry derry, perriwig, and a hatband,
> Hic hoc horum genitivo—

To be said in one breath.

124

Oh, my Ella—my blue bella,
A secula seculorum,
If I have luck, sir, she's my uxor,
O dies Benedictorum!

Or something about:

Sweet cowslips grace, the nominative case,
And She's of the feminine gender.

Days of Valpy the Vulture, eating the schoolboy's heart out, Eton Latin grammar, accidence—do not pause, traveller, if you see his tomb!

"Play to me," said Amaryllis, and the Fleet-Street man put away his pipe, and took up his flute; he breathed soft and low—an excellent thing in a musician—delicious airs of Mozart chiefly.

The summer unfolded itself at their knees, the high buttercups of the meadow came to the very door, the apple-bloom poured itself out before them; music all of it, music in colour, in light, in flowers, in song of happy birds. The soothing flute strung together the flow of their thoughts, they were very silent, Amaryllis and Amadis Iden—almost hand in hand—listening to his cunning lips.

He ceased, and they were still silent, listening to their own hearts.

The starlings flew by every few minutes to their nests in the thatch of the old house, and out again to the meadow.

Alere showed how impossible it was to draw a bird in flight by the starling's wings. His wings beat up and down so swiftly that the eye had not time to follow them completely; they formed a burr—an indistinct flutter; you are supposed to see the starling flying from you. The lifted tips were depressed so quickly that the impression of them in the raised position had not time to fade from the eye before a fresh impression arrived exhibiting them depressed to their furthest extent; you thus saw the wings in both positions, up and down, at once. A capital letter X may roughly represent his idea; the upper part answers to the wings lifted, the lower part to the wings down, and you see both together. Further, in actual fact, you see the wings in innumerable other positions between these two extremes; like the leaves of a book opened with your thumb quickly—as they do in legerdemain—almost as you see the spokes of a wheel run together as they revolve—a sort of burr.

To produce an image of a starling flying, you must draw all this.

125

The swift feathers are almost liquid; they leave a streak behind in the air like a meteor.

Thus the genial Goliath ale renewed the very blood in Alere's veins.

Amaryllis saw too that the deadly paleness of Amadis Iden's cheeks—absolute lack of blood—began to give way to the faintest colour, little more than the delicate pink of the apple-bloom, though he could take hardly a wine-glass of Goliath. If you threw a wine-glassful of the Goliath on the hearth it blazed up the chimney in the most lively manner. Fire in it—downright fire! That is the test.

Amadis could scarcely venture on a wine-glassful, yet a faint pink began to steal into his face, and his white lips grew moist. He drank deeply of another cup.

CHAPTER XXXII

LET me try," said Amadis, taking the handle of the churn from Jearje. The butter was obstinate, and would not come; it was eleven o'clock in the morning, and still there was the rattle of milk in the barrel, the sound of a liquid splashing over and over. By the sounds Mrs. Iden knew that the fairies were in the churn. Jearje had been turning for hours.

Amadis stooped to the iron handle, polished like silver by Jearje's rough hands—a sort of skin sand-paper—and with an effort made the heavy blue-painted barrel revolve on its axis.

Mrs. Iden, her sleeves up, looked from the dairy window into the court where the churn stood.

"Ah, it's no use your trying," she said, "you'll only tire yourself."

Jearje, glad to stand upright a minute, said, "First-rate, measter."

Amaryllis cried, "Take care; you'd better not, you'll hurt yourself."

"Aw!—aw!" laughed Bill Nye, who was sitting on a form by the wall under the dairy window. He was waiting to see Iden about the mowing. "Aw!—aw! Look 'ee thur, now!"

Heavily the blue barrel went round—thrice, four times, five

126

times; the colour mounted into Amadis's cheeks, not so much from the labour as the unwonted stooping; his breath came harder; he had to desist, and go and sit down on the form beside Bill Nye.

"I wish you would not do it," said Amaryllis. "You know you're not strong yet." She spoke as if she had been his mother or his nurse, somewhat masterfully and reproachfully.

"I'm afraid I'm not," said poor Amadis. His chin fell and his face lengthened—his eyes grew larger—his temples pinched; disappointment wrung at his heart.

Convalescence is like walking in sacks; a short waddle and a fall.

"I can tell 'ee of a vine thing, measter," said Bill Nye, "as I knows on; you get a pint measure full of snails——"

"There, do hold your tongue, it's enough to make anyone ill to think of," said Amaryllis, angrily, and Bill was silent as to the cod-liver oil virtues of snails. Amaryllis went to fetch a glass of milk for Amadis.

A robin came into the court, and perching on the edge of a tub, fluttered his wings, cried "Check, check," "Anything for me this morning?" and so put his head on one side, languishing and persuasive.

"My sister, as was in a decline, used to have snail-oil rubbed into her back," said Luce, the maid, who had been standing in the doorway with a duster.

"A pretty state of things," cried Mrs. Hen, in a passion. "You standing there doing nothing, and it's butter-making morning, and everything behind, and you idling and talking,"—rushing out from the dairy, and following Luce, who retreated indoors.

"Hur'll catch it," said Bill Nye.

"Missis is ——" said Jearje, supplying the blank with a wink, and meaning in a temper this morning. "Missis," like all nervous people, was always in a fury about nothing when her mind was intent on an object; in this case, the butter.

"Here's eleven o'clock," she cried, in the sitting-room, pointing to the clock, "and the beds ain't made."

"I've made the beds," said stolid Luce.

"And the fire isn't dusted up."

"I've dusted up the fire."

"And you're a lazy slut"—pushing Luce about the room.

"I bean't a lazy slut."

"You haven't touched the mantelpiece; give me the duster!"—snatching it from her.

"He be done."

"All you can do is to stand and talk with the men. There's no water taken up stairs."

"That there be."

"You know you ought to be doing something; the lazy lot of people in this house; I never saw anything like it; there's Mr. Iden's other boots to be cleaned, and there's the parlour to be swept, and the path to be weeded, and the things to be taken over for washing, and the teapot ought to go in to Woolhorton, you know the lid's loose, and the children will be here in a minute for the scraps, and your master will be in to lunch, and there's not a soul to help me in the least," and so, flinging the duster at Luce, out she flew into the court, and thence into the kitchen, where she cut a great slice of bread and cheese, and drew a quart of ale, and took them out to Bill Nye.

"Aw, thank'ee m'm," said Bill, from the very depth of his chest, and set to work happily.

Next, she drew a mug for Jearje, who held it with one hand and sipped, while he turned with the other; his bread and cheese he ate in like manner, he could not wait till he had finished the churning.

"Verily, man is made up of impatience," said the angel Gabriel in the Koran, as you no doubt remember; Adam was made of clay (who was the sculptor's ghost that modelled him?) and when the breath of life was breathed into him, he rose on his arm and began to eat before his lower limbs were yet vivified. This is a fact. "Verily, man is made up of impatience." As the angel had never had a stomach or anything to sit upon, as the French say, he need not have made so unkind a remark; if he had had a stomach and a digestion like Bill Nye and Jearje, it is certain he would never have wanted to be an angel.

Next, there were four cottage children now in the court, waiting for scraps.

Mrs. Iden, bustling to and fro like a whirlwind, swept the poor little things into the kitchen and filled two baskets for them with slices of bread and butter, squares of cheese, a beef bone, half a rabbit, a dish of cold potatoes, two bottles of beer from the barrel, odds and ends, and so swept them off again in a jiffy.

Mrs. Iden! Mrs. Iden! you ought to be ashamed of yourself, that is not the way to feed the poor. What could you be thinking of, you ignorant farmer's wife!

You should go to London, Mrs. Iden, and join a Committee with duchesses and earlesses, and wives of rich City tradesfolk; much more important these than the duchesses, they will teach you manners. They will teach you how to feed the poor with the help of the Rev. Joseph Speechify, and the scientific Dr. Amœba Bacillus; Joe has Providence at his fingers' ends, and guides it in the right way; Bacillus knows everything to a particle; with Providence and Science together they must do it properly.

The scientific dinner for the poor must be composed of the principles of food in the right proportion: (1) Albuminates, (2) Hydro-Carbons, (3) Carbo-hydrates. Something juicy coming now!

The scientific dinner consists of haricot beans, or lentil soup, or oatmeal porridge, or vegetable pot-bouilli; say twopence a quart. They can get all the proteids out of that, and lift the requisite foot-tons.

No wasteful bread and butter, no scandalous cheese, no abominable beef bone, no wretched rabbit, no prodigal potatoes, above all, No immoral ale!

There, Mrs. Iden.

Go to the famous Henry Ward Beecher, that shining light and apostle, Mrs. Iden, and read, mark, learn, and inwardly digest what he says:—

"A man who cannot live on bread is not fit to live. A family may live, laugh, love and be happy that eats bread in the morning with good water, and water and good bread at noon, and water and bread at night."

Does that sound like an echo of the voice that ceased on the Cross?

Guilty Mrs Iden, ignorant farmer's wife; hide your beef and ale, your rabbit and potatoes.

To duchesses and earlesses, and plump City ladies riding in carriages, and all such who eat and drink five times a day, and have six or eight courses at dinner, doubtless once now and then a meal of vegetable pot-bouilli, or oatmeal porridge, or lentil soup (three halfpence a pound lentils), or haricot beans and water would prove a scientifically wholesome thing.

But to those who exist all the week on hunches of dry bread, and not much of that, oatmeal porridge doesn't seem to come as a luxury. They would like something juicy; good rumpsteak now, with plenty of rich gravy, broad slices from legs of mutton, and foaming mugs of ale. They need something to put fresh blood and warmth into them.

You sometimes hear people remark: "How strange it is—the poor never buy oatmeal, or lentils!"

Of course they don't; if by any chance they do get a shilling to spend, they like a mutton chop. They have enough of farinaceous fare.

What Mrs. Iden ought to have done had she been scientific,

was to have given each of these poor hungry children a nicely printed little pamphlet, teaching them how to cook.

Instead of which, she set all their teeth going; infinitely wicked Mrs. Iden!

CHAPTER XXXIII

YOU must drink it all—every drop," said Amaryllis, masterfully, as Amadis lingered over the glass of milk she had brought him. He had but half finished it; she insisted, "Come, drink it all." Amadis made an effort, and obeyed.

But his heart was bitter as absinthe.

Everyone else was strong, and hardy, and manly; even the women were manly, they could eat and drink.

Rough-headed Jearje, at the churn, ate hard cheese, and drank ale, and turned the crank at the same time.

Round-headed Bill Nye sat on the form, happily munching cheese, oh so happily! Gabriel (of the Koran) would never believe how happily, sipping his tall quart-mug.

Mrs. Iden bustled to and fro, for all her fifty years, more energetic than all the hamlet put together.

Luce, the maid, had worked since six, and would go on hours longer.

Alere Flamma was smoking and sipping Goliath ale in the summer-house; he could eat, and drink, and walk about as a man should.

Amaryllis was as strong as a young lioness; he had seen her turn the heavy cheese-tub round as if it were a footstool.

He alone was weak, pale, contemptible; unable to eat strong meat; unable to drink strong drink; put down to sip milk as an infant; unable to walk farther than Plum Corner in the garden; unable to ride even; a mere shadow, a thing of contempt.

They told him he was better. There was just a trifle of pink in his face, and he could walk to Plum Corner in the garden without clinging to Amaryllis's arm, or staying to steady himself and get his balance more than three or four times. He had even ventured a little way up the meadow-path, but it made him giddy to stoop to pick a

130

buttercup. They told him he was better; he could eat a very little more, and sip a wine-glassful of Goliath.

Better! What a mockery to a man who could once row, and ride, and shoot, and walk his thirty miles, and play his part in any sport you chose! It was absinthe to him.

He could not stoop to turn the churn—he had to sip milk in the presence of strong men drinking strong drink; to be despised; the very servant-maid talking of him as in a decline.

And before Amaryllis; before whom he wished to appear a man.

And full of ideas, too; he felt that he had ideas, that he could think, yet he could scarce set one foot safely before the other, not without considering first and feeling his way.

Rough-headed Jearje, without a thought, was as strong as the horses he led in the waggon.

Round-headed Bill Nye, without an idea, could mow all day in the heat of July.

He, with all his ideas, his ambitions, his exalted hopes, his worship of Amaryllis—he was nothing. Less than nothing—a shadow.

To despise oneself is more bitter than absinthe.

Let us go to Al Hariri once again, and hear what he says. The speaker has been very, very ill, but is better:—

And he prostrated himself long in prayer: then raised his head, and said:—

"Despair not in calamities of a gladdening that shall wipe away thy sorrows;
For how many a simoom blows, then turns to a gentle breeze, and is changed!
How many a hateful cloud arises, then passes away, and pours not forth!
And the smoke of the wood, fear is conceived of it, yet no blaze appears from it;
And oft sorrow rises, and straightway sets again.
So be patient when fear assails, for Time is the Father of Wonders;
And hope from the peace of God blessings not to be reckoned!"

How should such a chant as this enter a young man's heart who felt himself despicable in the sight of his mistress?

"Should you like a little more?" asked Amaryllis, in a very gentle tone, now he had obeyed her.

"I would rather not," said Amadis, still hanging his head.

His days were mixed of honey and wormwood; sweet because of Amaryllis, absinthe because of his weakness.

131

A voice came from the summer-house; Flamma was shouting an old song, with heavy emphasis here and there, with big capital letters:—

The jolly old Sun, where goes he at night?
And what does he Do, when he's out of Sight?
All Insinuation Scorning;
I don't mean to Say that he Tipples apace,
I only Know he's a very Red Face
When he gets up in the Morning!

"Haw! Haw! Haw!" laughed Bill Nye, with his mouth full. "Th' zun do look main red in the marning, surely."

They heard the front door open and shut; Iden had come in for his lunch, and, by the sound of the footsteps, had brought one of his gossips with him.

At this Mrs. Iden began to ruffle up her feathers for battle.

Iden came through into the dairy.

"Now, you ain't wanted here," she said. "Poking your nose into everything. Wonder you don't help Luce make the beds and sweep the floor!"

"Can I help'ee?" said Iden, soothingly. "Want any wood for the fire—or anything?"

"As if Luce couldn't fetch the wood—and chop it, as well as you. Why can't you mind your business? Here's Bill Nye been waiting these two hours to see you"—following Iden towards the sitting-room. "Who have you brought in with you now? Of course, everybody comes in of a butter-making morning, just the busiest time! Oh! it's you! Sit still, Mr. Duck; I don't mind you. What will you take?"

More ale and cheese here, too; Iden and Jack Duck sat in the bow-window and went at their lunch. So soon as they were settled, out flounced Mrs. Iden into the dairy: "The lazy lot of people in this house—I never saw anything like it!"

It was true.

There was Alere Flamma singing in the summer-house; Amadis Iden resting on the form; Amaryllis standing by him; Bill Nye munching; Jearje indolently rotating the churn with one hand, and feeding himself with the other; Luce sitting down to her lunch in the kitchen; Iden lifting his mug in the bow-window; Jack Duck with his great mouth full; eight people—and four little children trotting down the road with baskets of food.

"The lazy lot of people in this house; I never saw anything like it."

And that was the beauty of the place, the "Let us not trouble ourselves;" "a handful in Peace and Quiet" is better than set banquets; crumbs for everybody, and for the robin too; "God listens to those who pray to him. Let us eat, and drink, and think of nothing;" believe me, the plain plenty, and the rest, and peace, and sunshine of an old farmhouse, there is nothing like it in this world!

"I never saw anything like it. Nothing done; nothing done; the morning gone and nothing done; and the butter's not come yet!"

Homer is thought much of; now, his heroes are always eating. They eat all through the Iliad, they eat at Patroclus' tomb; Ulysses eats a good deal in the Odyssey: Jupiter eats. They only did at Coombe-Oaks as was done on Olympus.

CHAPTER XXXIV

AMARYLLIS went outside the court, and waited; Amadis rose and followed her. "Come a little way into the Brook-Field," she said.

They left the apple-bloom behind them, and going down the gravel-path passed the plum trees—the daffodils there were over now—by the strawberry patch which Iden had planted under the parlour window; by the great box-hedge where a thrush sat on her nest undisturbed, though Amaryllis's dress brushed the branches; by the espalier apple, to the little orchard-gate.

The parlour-window—there are no parlours now, except in old country houses; there were parlours in the days of Queen Anne; in the modern villas they have drawing-rooms.

The parlour-window hung over with pear-tree branches, planted beneath with strawberry; white blossom above, white flower beneath; birds' nests in the branches of the pear—that was Iden.

They opened the little orchard-gate which pushed heavily against the tall meadow-grass growing between the bars. The path was almost gone—grown out with grass, and as they moved they left a broad trail behind them.

Bill Nye the mower, had he seen, would have muttered to himself; they were trespassing on his mowing-grass, trampling it, and making it more difficult to cut.

Her dress swept over the bennets and shook the thick-stemmed butter-cups—branched like the golden candlestick, and with flowers of golden flame. For the burnished petals reflect the sun, and throw light back into the air.

Amadis began to drag behind—he could not walk much farther; they sat down together on the trunk of an oak that had been felled by a gateway close to the horse-chestnut trees Iden had planted. Even with his back leaning against a limb of the oak, Amadis had to partly support himself with his hands.

What was the use of such a man?—He had nothing but his absurdly romantic name from Don Quixote to recommend him.

That was the very thought that gnawed at poor Amadis's heart as he sat by her side. What use to care for him?

Iden's flag-basket of tools lay by the gate, it was a new gate, and he had been fitting it before he went in to lunch. His basket was of flag because the substance of the flag is soft, and the tools, chisels, and so on, laid pleasant in it; he must have everything right. The new gate was of solid oak, no "sappy" stuff, real heart of oak, well-seasoned, without a split, fine, close-grained timber, cut on the farm, and kept till it was thoroughly fit, genuine English oak. If you would only consider Iden's gate you might see there the man.

This gateway was only between two meadows, and the ordinary farmer, when the old gate wore out, would have stopped it with a couple of rails, or a hurdle or two, something very, very cheap and rough; at most a gate knocked up by the village carpenter of ash and willow, at the lowest possible charge.

Iden could not find a carpenter good enough to make his gate in the hamlet; he sent for one ten miles, and paid him full carpenter's wages. He was not satisfied then, he watched the man at his work to see that the least little detail was done correctly, till the fellow would have left the job, had he not been made pliable by the Goliath ale. So he just stretched the job out as long as he could, and talked and talked with Iden, and stroked him the right way, and drank the ale, and "played it upon me and on William, That day in a way I despise." Till what with the planing, and shaving, and smoothing, and morticing, and ale, and time, it footed up a pretty bill, enough for three commonplace gates, not of the Iden style.

Why, Iden had put away those pieces of timber years before for this very purpose, and had watched the sawyers saw them out at the pit. They would have made good oak furniture. There was nothing special or particular about this gateway; he had done the same in turn for every gateway on the farm; it was the Iden way.

A splendid gate it was, when it was finished, fit for a nobleman's Home Park. I doubt, if you would find such a gate, so well proportioned, and made of such material on any great estate in the kingdom. For not even dukes can get an Iden to look after their property. An Iden is not to be "picked up," I can tell you.

The neighbourhood round about had always sneered in the broad country way at Iden's gates. "Vit for m' Lard's park. What do he want wi' such geates? A' ain't a got no cattle to speak on; any ould rail ud do as good as thuck geat."

The neighbourhood round about could never understand Iden, never could see why he had gone to such great trouble to render the homestead beautiful with trees, why he had re-planted the orchard with pleasant eating apples in the place of the old cider apples, hard and sour. "Why wouldn't thaay a' done for he as well as for we?"

All the acts of Iden seemed to the neighbourhood to be the acts of a "vool."

When he cut a hedge, for instance, Iden used to have the great bushes that bore unusually fine May bloom saved from the billhook, that they might flower in the spring. So, too, with the crab-apples—for the sake of the white blossom; so, too, with the hazel—for the nuts.

But what caused the most "wonderment" was the planting of the horse-chestnuts in the corner of the meadow? Whatever did he want with horse-chestnuts? No other horse-chestnuts grew about there. You couldn't eat the horse-chestnuts when they dropped in autumn.

In truth Iden built for all time, and not for the little circumstance of the hour. His gate was meant to last for years, rain and shine, to endure any amount of usage, to be a work of Art in itself.

His gate as the tangible symbol of his mind—was at once his strength and his folly. His strength, for it was such qualities as these that made Old England famous, and set her on the firm base whereon she now stands—built for all Time. His folly, because he made too much of little things, instead of lifting his mind higher.

If only he could have lived three hundred years the greater world would have begun to find out Iden and to idolize him, and make pilgrimages from over sea to Coombe Oaks, to hear him talk, for Iden could talk of the trees and grass, and all that the Earth bears, as if one had conversed face to face with the great god Pan himself.

But while Iden slumbered with his head against the panel—think, think, think—this shallow world of ours, this petty threescore years and ten, was slipping away. Already Amaryllis had marked with bitterness at heart the increasing stoop of the strong back.

Iden was like the great engineer who could never build a bridge, because he knew so well how a bridge ought to be built.

"Such a fuss over a mess of a gate," said Mrs. Iden, "making yourself ridiculous: I believe that carpenter is just taking advantage of you. Why can't you go into town and see your father?—it would be a hundred pounds in your pocket"—as it would have been, no doubt. If only Mrs. Iden had gone about her lecture in a pleasanter manner perhaps he would have taken her advice.

Resting upon the brown timber in the grass Amaryllis and Amadis could just see a corner of the old house through the spars of the new gate. Coombe Oaks was a grown house, if you understand; a house that had grown in the course of many generations, not built to set order; it had grown like a tree that adapts itself to circumstances, and, therefore, like the tree it was beautiful to look at. There were windows in deep notches, between gables where there was no look-out except at the pears on the wall, awkward windows, quite bewildering. A workman came to mend one one day, and could not get at it. "Darned if I ever seed such a crooked picter of a house!" said he.

A kingfisher shot across above the golden surface of the buttercups, straight for the brook, moving, as it seemed, without wings, so swiftly did he vibrate them, that only his azure hue was visible, drawn like a line of peacock blue over the gold.

In the fitness of things Amaryllis ought not to have been sitting there like this, with Amadis lost in the sweet summer dream of love.

She ought to have loved and married a Launcelot du Lake, a hero of the mighty arm, only with the income of Sir Gorgius Midas: that is the proper thing.

But the fitness of things never comes to pass—everything happens in the Turkish manner.

Here was Amaryllis, very strong and full of life, very, very young and inexperienced, very poor and without the least expectation whatever (for who could reconcile the old and the older Iden?), the daughter of poor and embarrassed parents, whom she wished and prayed to help in their coming old age. Here was Amaryllis, full of poetic feeling and half a painter at heart, full of generous sentiments—what a nature to be ground down in the sordidness of married poverty!

Here was Amadis, extremely poor, quite feeble, and unable to earn a shilling, just talking of seeing the doctor again about this fearful debility, full too, as he thought at least, of ideas—what a being to think of her!

Nothing ever happens in the fitness of things. If only now he could have regained the health and strength of six short months ago—if only that, but you see, he had not even that. He might get better; true—he might, I have tried 80 drugs and I am no better, I hope he will.

Could any blundering Sultan in the fatalistic East have put things together for them with more utter contempt of fitness? It is all in the Turkish manner, you see.

There they sat, happier and happier, and deeper and deeper in love every moment, on the brown timber in the long grass, their hearts as full of love as the meadow was of sunshine.

You have heard of the Sun's Golden Cup, in which after sunset he was carried over Ocean's stream, while we slumber in the night, to land again in the East and give us the joy of his rising. The great Golden Cup in which Hercules, too, was taken over; it was as if that Cup had been filled to the brim with the nectar of love and placed at the lips to drink, inexhaustible.

In the play of Faust—Alere's Faust—Goethe has put an interlude, an Intermezzo; I shall leave Amaryllis and Amadis in their Interlude in Heaven. Let the Play of Human Life, with its sorrows and its Dread, pause awhile; let Care go aside behind the wings, let Debt and Poverty unrobe, let Age stand upright, let Time stop still (oh, Miracle! as the Sun did in the Vale of Ajalon). Let us leave our lovers in the Interlude in Heaven.

And as I must leave them (I trust but for a little while) I will leave them on the brown oak timber, sap-stain brown, in the sunshine and dancing shadow of summer, among the long grass and the wild flowers.